English Lessons

Books by J.M. Hayes

Mad Dog & Englishman Mysteries
Mad Dog & Englishman
Prairie Gothic
Plains Crazy
Broken Heartland
Server Down
English Lessons

Other Mysteries
The Grey Pilgrim

English Lessons

A Mad Dog &
Englishman Mystery

J. M. Hayes

Poisoned Pen Press

Copyright © 2011 by J. M. Hayes

First Edition 2011

10 9 8 7 6 5 4 3 2 1

Library of Congress Catalog Card Number: 2011920313

ISBN: 9781590589151   Hardcover
       9781590589175   Trade Paperback

Poisoned Pen Press
6962 E. First Ave., Ste. 103
Scottsdale, AZ 85251
www.poisonedpenpress.com
info@poisonedpenpress.com

Printed in the United States of America

For my greats—
Brice, Kyle, Christi, Tracy,
Andrew, Matthew, & Justin.
May you make a world with
no need for guns and no place for bigots.

I remember America,
I remember it well,
When you could walk downtown in the middle of the night
Without the smell of fear on your shoulder
As you jump at every sound
And you never look in the eye of any stranger
Who could easily gun you down.
I remember America,
I remember every town,
When crack was the sound that caps would make
In the only guns kids would have around.

—John Stewart (1939–2008)
"I Remember America"

The governor-elect of Arizona smiled at Officer Heather English, though it took some help from a gust of wind to pucker his cheeks and lift the corners of his mouth. That was because his skin had been tacked to a weathered wooden wall to cure. Upside down, though the wind lifted and twisted his face so Heather could recognize it. She might not have done so, even then, since the bone structure beneath the skin is critical in giving a face its shape. Soon-to-be Governor Joe Hyde—and Heather was quick to note the irony of his name and his current condition—had dramatic wavy locks and an odd, twin-pointed beard. Heather had only seen two like it. One on this man. The other, on photographs of Sir Richard Francis Burton, nineteenth-century explorer of holy cities and dark continents. A star-shaped scar above the right eyebrow matched Hyde, not Burton, so this fleshless face, and the mostly hairless pelt attached to it, must, she realized, belong to the governor.

Heather was not thrilled at encountering Arizona's new governor here, not that she would have cared to meet him any time. He was a law-and-order camera-ready sheriff who'd run an independent campaign in the last election and won, apparently, because a vote for him was seen by most as a vote for "neither of the above."

Arizona was conservative, but Hyde flew to the right of the average emperor. Hyde had run his county like a private fiefdom for the benefit of himself and his friends. He'd campaigned against both parties, promised tax cuts for everyone, guaranteed he'd seal the border, and planned to round up every illegal alien for immediate deportation.

Xenophobia was popular along the border these days. Experts claimed his administration would wreck the state's already fragile economy. Voters hadn't cared. And Hyde had suggested God should visit the most terrible of deaths upon him if he ever lied to the electorate. Let him suffer the worst anguish of any of the saints or martyrs if he failed to govern wisely. Heather wondered if someone had taken Hyde up on the proposal, choosing the fate of Saint Bartholomew, who was said to have been flayed alive and crucified upside down. If not, perhaps someone who expected to be skinned by the governor's policies had made a pre-emptive strike.

As a Sewa Tribal Police Officer, Heather English preferred not to see even the most incompetent politicians assassinated. Recalled, was more to her taste. Worse, she was the first law enforcement officer on the scene. Hyde's assassination was going to be big. Every network would jump aboard this story, 24/7. It would take something apocalyptic to knock Hyde's bizarre murder from the headlines. Some talking heads had begun passing along the governor's thoughtless ramblings as if they were mighty truths issued straight from a burning bush—speaking of his inevitable run for the presidency.

Oh, God. This would make her life a nightmare. But then it hadn't done much for Hyde, either.

The call had come in at six last night. According to an anonymous tipster, someone with no business on the reservation was working an old mine in this canyon.

Truly anonymous tips were hard to get these days, unless you used a pay phone on the Mexican side of the border, as this informant had.

Times were tough. The price of gold had skyrocketed as fast as jobs disappeared. Even this lonely spot, long believed to have been mined out, might produce enough ore to make trespassing on the Sewa Reservation worth the risk. According to the caller, the miner always hit on weekends and holidays. And so the report went on the list—something to be checked out as soon as an officer could be spared. Lucky Heather was that officer.

Being a Sewa Tribal Police officer wasn't everything she'd expected. Her father was a Kansas sheriff. She'd lived around law enforcement all her life, understood the majority of her job would be sorting out minor arguments, misunderstandings, and family or neighbor fights. Some of those could get nasty. And she'd known her life would be most at risk when she was untangling domestic disputes involving alcohol and firearms. Because of her father's career, she'd been better prepared for the job than the average rookie. But this was a tribal police force. And she wasn't a member of the tribe. There were still hard feelings about that. Some people on the force hadn't forgiven her for being marginally Cheyenne instead of fully Sewa. Especially when she looked about as Anglo-All-American girl-next-door as possible—light complexion, hair color pale enough to seem blond among Sewas, a sprinkle of freckles, sparkling eyes more green than hazel. "The White Girl" was what they called her behind her back. Some of them said it to her face.

So she asked for the dirty jobs. Took the holiday weekends. Did her best to be low profile, but a solid performer. Most of them still had little use for her. That was why she was out here doing a steep hike through a lonely canyon on Christmas morning. It would get worse now, once word got around that "The White Girl" had stepped into the prime spot in the biggest case the Sewa Tribal Police had ever faced. Between the ravenous press and a lot of fellow officers who'd be happy to get her fired, she was going to be under the microscope.

Those thoughts flashed through Heather's mind in the moment between recognizing Governor Hyde and realizing there was an envelope lying at the foot of the wall on which he hung. It was secured from the day's cool breezes by a fist-sized rock.

You found a murder victim, you started by making sure the murderer wasn't still around.

Heather didn't think so. Nor anyone else. The wall Hyde decorated was the only one still standing. She'd noticed it as she hiked up into the canyon. And the curiosity of a single wall out here in the middle of nowhere had drawn her through the thickets of scrub mesquite that lined the dry wash at the canyon's center. In getting to the wall, she had climbed past the canyon's best hiding places. Still, she drew her weapon from her holster. If this were an off-duty hike, she'd have left the gun in her vehicle, a couple of miles back where the road had been washed out a few storms ago. From that point on it was just a rough trail. A track—too rugged and strewn with boulders for her to be sure whether anyone had been up here recently, though she hadn't seen any signs.

Heather didn't like guns much, but this one felt reassuring as it filled her hand. SIG-Sauer P-226. She might not like it, but she was good with it. She consistently shot the best scores on the Sewa police range. Another reason some of the fellows weren't thrilled to have her around. She might try to keep a low profile, but she wouldn't intentionally miss a target just to reassure the guys she worked with that they had big *cojones*.

She had begun to fall in love with this oddly lush desert that was her new home. A day of solitude appreciating jagged mountains, thorny brush, prickly cactus, and warm December sun while she convinced a twenty-first-century prospector to give up his diggings had seemed a perfect alternative to the normal excess of food and gifts. A good way to spend a Christmas half-way across the country from most of her family and refocus on the things she loved about this job, and why she'd moved a thousand miles to take it. Only there were clouds instead of sun, the high thin kind that made for spectacular sunsets but offered no chance of rain. A cool breeze blew away the warmth. And, what she had found here had nothing to do with a simple eviction notice.

She drew her cell to report her discovery and ask for back-up. Her cell showed not a single bar. That's the way it worked in the Arizona wilds. Too many mountains. Too many empty places without enough customers—places like the Sewa Reservation. She didn't have a radio with her. There was one down in her unit—the tribal force couldn't afford redundant systems. Cells were cheap and fast and worked just fine unless you were out in the boonies. In fact, her cell might work if she hiked up the side of the canyon to a crest. But before she did that, she had to secure the crime scene. From whom, she wondered? But she had found i, and they would come. Besides, those were the rules.

She pulled a role of tape out of her fanny pack and roped off a big circle around the governor. The thorns on the plants she used to establish a perimeter meant she didn't have to waste a lot of time with fancy knots. Other than Hyde's hide and the envelope, Heather still saw no signs that anyone had been here since that wall was abandoned. No footprints, even though there was enough sand in the rocky soil to show the tracks she'd left climbing in. Well, she could document that. She pulled out her cell phone to take pictures.

She began with several of Hyde taken from a variety of angles to show how the skin had been nailed to the wall and that there was no evidence of significant trauma to it, other than being skinned. And that there were no footprints nearby except hers. She photographed one of her prints and the pattern on the sole of her shoe to make that clear. She backtracked down to the wash, looking for others. There were some scuffs, but nothing with a clear outline. She photographed them anyway.

Next, she moved in on the skin for close-ups. There were some scrapes, and a few old scars. Some marks on the hands that might have been defensive wounds. She turned them all into jpegs. She took no close ups of Hyde's sex organs. There was nothing remarkable about them and no evidence he'd been molested there—not since his circumcision, anyway.

Finally, the envelope. She got out a plastic evidence bag and a pair of latex gloves. She lifted the rock and dropped it in a bag. The wind immediately picked up the envelope and tumbled it into a clump of scraggly desert broom. She retrieved it. There was a neatly printed name—ink jet, most likely—on the front of the envelope. No great surprise. That the name was "Heather English," however, was another matter entirely.

◇◇◇

A thousand miles northeast, it was noon and Sheriff English had done all the laundry, vacuuming, and dusting he could stand. His house was too big and too empty. He would never get used to that. His wife, Judy, had been dead for six Christmases now. And his daughters, though usually home for the holidays, had begun attending college and living in distant places even before that. This year, his daughters weren't here to help cut the loneliness. One was a tribal police officer in southern Arizona and on duty today. The other was wrapping up her dissertation because an honest-to-God paying faculty position waited for her next fall if she met her deadlines and scored that Ph.D. on schedule in the spring. So, this Christmas, the empty house was getting to him.

He flipped on the TV for companionable noise and decided he couldn't handle *It's a Wonderful Life* again, or even an alternative holiday "classic" like *Die Hard*. So, though he wouldn't get paid for working on Christmas, he let himself out of the house, climbed behind the wheel of Judy's old Taurus, and headed for the office to do paperwork.

Actually, the question of getting paid for working Christmas hardly concerned him. Benteen County, Kansas, never an economic dynamo of the Plains, was in the middle of something resembling a full-scale depression at the moment. The county owed him six months' back pay, which he would have been demanding if he and Judy hadn't been smart enough to set up a trust fund to pay for their daughters' educations. Claiming the money would also probably cost him the only two employees he had left. Losing Deputy Wynn wouldn't matter much. About all Wynn was good for was warm-body duty. But Mrs. Kraus, his office manager, was irreplaceable. She knew everything about everybody in the county. More than once, she'd talked an emergency situation down into a call that didn't even have to be answered, and not just because there was no one to answer it.

Today's paperwork involved his department's budget. Deputy Wynn and Mrs. Kraus hadn't been paid up to date either. And one of the perks of his office was supposed to be the use of the county's black and white. Except it was in the shop waiting for the board of supervisors to fund the replacement of a blown head gasket. Or perhaps something worse, once a mechanic pulled the head and discovered the true extent of twelve years and 380,000 miles of wear. He wanted it back, though, because strangers didn't respect an old Taurus station wagon as a legitimate vehicle of law enforcement, even with the temporary light bar he'd strapped across its roof.

He didn't get to the courthouse. As soon as he reached Veteran's Memorial Park he realized there was a disturbance at the Buffalo Springs Nondenominational Church. A two-tone tan Ford Torino of mid-seventies vintage was trying to back out into the street from where it had been parked beside the church. Trying was the operative word. As was failing.

Kansas weather had been typical the last few weeks. Warm one day, bitterly cold the next. With occasional rain, sleet, and snow between brief moments of bright sun. The soil alternated back and forth between mud bog and diamond-hard dirty ice. It had been warm and melting yesterday morning. Then another cold front blew through, blessing the county with frozen puddles, black ice, and a couple of inches of fresh snow. The thermometer was hovering around zero this bleak, gray Christmas morning, reminding folks of one more reason to move away from Kansas if the economy ever improved enough to give them another chance.

Apparently the slight rise between the church and the street had frozen into an insurmountable obstacle, at least for the Torino. The car's owner lived at the end of the sheriff's block, and the edge of town. She was the proverbial little old lady—prim, proper, and looking as sweet as the honey her husband had harvested from the hives their back yard held before he passed away. Except when she had a nasty rumor to spread or lost her always fragile hold on the temper the sheriff thought had helped send her husband to an early grave. The frustration of failing to back into the street had evidently unleashed that temper again. In a big way, if the scrapes and dents her Torino accumulated as it played bumper pool with the cars parked on either side were an indication. Their horrified owners shouted for her to stop, as did a considerable portion of the congregation, all of them discreetly behind the vehicles she kept ramming.

The sheriff parked his Taurus behind her. Since that was where she had been unsuccessfully trying to go for several minutes, it seemed the safest place. He got out of his car, considered the slick footing, and reluctantly reached back inside for his cane.

Most counties would have replaced a crippled sheriff, even one who had taken a bullet in the line of duty—a fragment that chipped the sheriff's spine and was putting him through a gruelingly slow recovery process. He was finally walking reasonably well, when the weather permitted. But there was no sense in risking further injury, not on snow and ice and in the vicinity of a crazed driver.

"Stop her, Sheriff," someone shouted.

"Look what she's done to my car," another parishioner complained.

"Mrs. Walker, turn off your ignition," the sheriff called.

Lottie Walker hunkered down in the seat and shoved the accelerator to the floor. The back wheels whined in slush of their own creation and she skewed into what had been an attractive Acura until moments ago. She must have thought she might still make a clean getaway if she could only reach the street. As if there were another Torino of this color combination and vintage with which she might be confused in the county, maybe even the entire Great Plains.

The sheriff drew his gun but the tires didn't slow any. The Torino slalomed over into an old Chevy that was receiving its own share of body damage. The sheriff limped across the berm that prevented her exit, and headed for the church building on the far side of the Acura. The crowd, suddenly silent, parted in front of him. He used the space between the Acura and the wall to get more or less in front of Mrs. Walker's Torino.

"I'm only going to ask you to shut the car off this one last time," he yelled, lowering the barrel of his .38 until it was aimed at the wobbling Ford. Mrs. Walker had slouched down even farther. He could only see the top of her favorite

Sunday-go-to-meeting hat, the one with the artificial rose jauntily affixed on one side. The Torino didn't stop.

The sheriff used his cane to get down on his hands and knees. If she suddenly put the car in drive instead of reverse, things could get seriously unpleasant for him. She didn't, though. And he got low enough to get a bead on her oil pan at an angle where the bullet would have to pass through her flywheel without harming anyone. He was fresh out of armor-iercing rounds, so that wasn't going to happen.

By the time he climbed back to his feet, hot oil melted the snow under her car and the engine made unpleasant noises.

"Best stand well back," the sheriff said. "Might throw a rod through the side of the block."

The engine threw something, though not where anyone could see it, and the back wheels suddenly stopped dead. The car slid slowly back into the spot it had been trying to leave. Mrs. Walker looked frantically around the inside of her car.

"Where's my purse?" Her question was clear even through closed windows.

"I've got it," Eldridge Beaumont said, stepping up to the front of the crowd and showing it to her. "You left it in the church."

Mrs. Walker adjusted her rose-adorned hat. Pointed an accusing finger at the sheriff.

"Mr. Beaumont, you are to sue Sheriff English and this county for the damages done to my classic antique automobile," she said.

Beaumont nodded.

"Good," English told her. "Maybe you can talk to Eldridge about that while he gives you a ride home. The two of you can also discuss restitution to the people who own these vehicles. And how you'll plead to the charges from the book I'm about to throw at you."

The sheriff might have begun listing them but his cell rang. He put his pistol away and answered it.

"Sheriff English," he said.

It was Mrs. Kraus.

"We got a problem, Englishman."

"I know," he said. "I'm in the middle of it."

"Nah, that slow motion accident in the church yard ain't nothin'. I just got a call—murder threat."

◇◇◇

Mad Dog gently ran the obsidian blade across a flap of skin. The blade was sharper than a scalpel and the skin offered no more resistance than butter. But, instead of the neat buckskin string he wanted, the result was wavy, uneven, and likely to break the first time he tied a knot in it.

Mad Dog wiped the sweat out of his eyes. The sweat probably hadn't helped, though what should he expect while sitting in a sweat lodge? Disgusted, he put the skin and his obsidian blade back in their storage box.

The buckskin had been a gift. Mad Dog didn't hunt anymore. He preferred to coexist with wildlife, not kill it. Not that he would try to argue someone else out of hunting. And he was no vegan. He simply didn't want to kill things anymore. He knew his no-kill, meat-eating lifestyle was inconsistent, but he'd stopped worrying about living a perfect life. The best he could do would have to be good enough.

For instance, he'd attended Christmas Eve services with Pam last night. And they had a tree and a few lights around their front door. All this in spite of the fact he wasn't a Christian. He was Cheyenne, though his bloodline was thin. Even so, he'd spent years trying to learn his people's ancient beliefs and master the skills of the shaman. That was why he was in a sweat lodge on Christmas morning. To purify himself.

Purification hadn't come easily, but boredom had. That was why he'd decided to work on making a medicine bundle. Half a dozen cuts had produced not one piece of useable string.

Everything in its time and place, he told himself. He sprinkled a little water on the stones to produce more steam and crumbled a bit of sage over the coals.

A vehicle pulled in around the front of the house and honked its horn. Mad Dog couldn't imagine who it might be. Pam was at work today, playing jazzy Christmas carols at the piano bar for holiday gamblers at the Sewa tribe's casino. She hadn't tried to get out of it. Holiday players tipped well.

It wouldn't be his niece, Heather, either. She wouldn't honk, and besides, she was on duty. Mad Dog and Pam had lived in this house in southern Arizona south of Three Points long enough to build a small circle of friends. But not the sort who dropped by unannounced on Christmas Day. What it sounded like was a delivery truck, but who delivered on Christmas?

Mad Dog threw open the blankets that covered his sweat lodge. He was a big man, and though he was beginning to show his years he still had more muscle than fat. The years might have shown more clearly in his hair, but he didn't have any. When he'd decided to live as a Cheyenne, he'd tried growing his hair out for braids. Naturally curly hair didn't make good braids, so he shaved it all off and stuck to that look instead.

It wasn't cold out, not by the Kansas standards he'd grown up with. He hadn't brought a robe, so he just slipped on his pair of flip-flops and shuffled around the outside of the house in his Speedo. It wasn't a big house, maybe a thousand square feet of doublewide, a place to stay while they looked for something permanent.

Finding a suitable rental wasn't easy when one of its occupants would be a wolf. Or wolf-hybrid. Not that Hailey hung around all the time. In fact, he had no idea where she'd gone this morning.

The vehicle that had honked was already gone by the time Mad Dog reached the front yard. Something brown and boxy disappeared in its own dust down their unpaved street. There was a package on the front porch. UPS, Mad Dog decided, though he was surprised they delivered on Christmas.

A plain brown shoe box sealed with packing tape and without an address label sat beside his front door. That ruled out UPS or one of their competitors. But the package was for him. Bright-red, felt-tip letters covered the lid. "Merry Christmas, Mad Dog!" they proclaimed.

A cool breeze ruffled the mesquites and reminded Mad Dog he was bathed in sweat and nearly naked. He picked up the box, opened the door, and stepped inside. The living room was on the right. The Christmas tree, a Charlie Brown special, stood in front of the window. There were still several packages under it. Pam had wrapped empty boxes to make their holiday season seem more festive and richer. Things were a little tight for them just now. She'd moved from Las Vegas after losing her job there. He hadn't wanted to go back to Kansas. Not after his house there burned to the ground. He was still waiting for the insurance company to come through. He'd expected to have to fight them for the money, but they'd made things even tougher by going chapter eleven, their contribution to a slumping economy. He was beginning to wonder if he'd get back anything at all.

Mad Dog knew he should shower and get into warm dry clothes, yet curiosity demanded he open the box.

Their living room didn't contain much furniture. A couple of second-hand recliners, a sofa, a TV, and a desk and chair over by the fake fireplace. He went to the desk. He'd emptied his pockets there last night and his pocket knife lay in the middle of a small heap of spare change. He used it to slit the tape enough to pop the lid off the package.

A gold signet ring protruded from the center of an assortment of colored tissue paper. The engraved surface bore the image of a curving snake. A feathered one, he saw, as he bent to look at it more closely.

He needed better light and his reading glasses. He pulled the ring out of the box. It didn't come up as easily as expected because it was still on a finger attached to a hand that had been severed at the wrist.

"Urk," Mad Dog said. He dropped it. The hand fell into the Christmas tree's branches where it seemed to grasp them just as desperately as Mad Dog tried to avoid barfing up breakfast.

◇◇◇

Heather's climb to the top of the ridge above the old mining camp proved harder than she expected. The slope was steep. The rock, fractured by extremes of heat and cold, crumbled underfoot. What little soil she encountered was even less stable and full of small spiny plants. They were always in her way and tended to snag when she passed, as if reluctant to let any living creature go by without inflicting pain. When she reached the top she found her cell had only one bar. She tried a series of numbers, beginning with tribal police headquarters, but failed to get through to any. In the end, the effort wasted almost half an hour without getting the word out and added the climb down to the distance she would have to hike back to her unit.

The only thing she'd gained was time to think about the letter and the crime scene and how all this related to her.

Who could possibly have known she'd be here? A couple of other officers had heard her volunteer to take this unwelcome assignment. She'd called Brad. They were supposed to have Christmas dinner with his folks tonight up in the foothills. It was a loose arrangement, though, since an assignment like this made it impossible for her to know when she could log out for the day. Then the drive up from the reservation and across Tucson always took forever.

Finding Hyde had sucked all the good feeling away from her morning. She'd started with quite a lot of that, after getting laid, good and proper, last night. Brad was special. The sex, great. She'd hoped for more tonight. Fond memories and anticipation had made her morning warmer and more pleasant than reality. Until she found the skin. Now, she'd settle for a soothing hug or, better yet, contacting someone for help with this crime scene.

Her boss, Captain Matus, could supply that help. He was one of the people who knew she was out here. He'd told her there were marvelous petroglyphs a couple of hundred yards above the old mine. No time to check them out, now.

None of the people who knew she was here, whether law enforcement officers or the attorney she was dating, would have had anything to do with this murder. So how had the person who left the envelope known she'd be the one who'd find it? Or had he simply wanted the enclosed message delivered to her when Hyde's remains were discovered?

The contents of the envelope didn't make that clear, though they seemed to indicate someone wanted her to get the message soon.

About half way back to her car she tried her cell again and, again, had no success. She took a moment to re-examine the letter.

You're not in Kansas anymore.

That made it clear the message really was for her, Kansas transplant that she was. Besides, she was the only Heather English serving on the Sewa Tribal Police Force.

Sonora, south of the Sewa Reservation, belongs to *el Perro Rabioso*—the Rabid Dog. The competing drug lords on either side of him have joined forces to split his territory. Hyde promised to make the border porous for *Rabioso*. Hyde could have been useful to those who plan to replace *Rabioso*, but the bosses don't work that way. They lack finesse, but they're effective at achieving results through high body counts. Hyde is a message to *Rabioso*, and Arizona politicians profiting from the drug trade—get out of our way. In case that message is too subtle, they intend to send others. You must try to stop them as they work their way up to *Rabioso*. Not just because it's your job. They'll begin with *Rabioso's* enforcers. *Rabioso's* right-hand man, *el Serpiente Emplumada*, is a virtual certainty. Each of these men is a killer many times over. They deserve what happens to them. But you must try to save them because you and I will test ourselves against each other soon. When that happens, you must be ready, deserving of the honor of facing me. That won't matter to you. But something else will. *Rabioso* knows he's under attack, so he moved north of the border and went into hiding in Tucson. Those who are after him think they've found him. Someone told them *Rabioso* is hiding in Three Points and has shaved his head. *Rabioso*, translated into English, is Mad Dog.

The letter, like the envelope, appeared to have been printed by a computer. There was no signature. Unless you counted the smiley face beneath the last line.

◇◇◇

Brad Cole stood in the reception area of Tucson International Airport watching the screen that showed arriving passengers descending from the security area. Niki bounced into view, paused, winked at the camera, and blew him a kiss. Every male passenger around Niki looked at his sister instead of the camera. The men beside Brad all seemed to stop breathing for a moment. Niki was pretty, but she had something more than looks. Something indefinable that made her command every stage. She was the little sister whose spunky approach to life he could never match, and yet he adored her. Everybody adored her. Before he finished the thought, she ran into his arms. Every guy in the waiting area envied him, even if he only got a sisterly hug and peck on the cheek.

"How's my hero?" Niki held him by the shoulders and stepped back for an appraising look.

"Exhausted from saving the world, of course," Brad laughed. "Otherwise, good."

"You look good," Niki decided. "Happy, even."

And to his surprise, Brad discovered that was how he felt—happy.

"I didn't check any luggage," Niki said. "Where are we parked?"

Taking charge, as usual. That was his little sister. She probably expected to drive.

He led the way toward short-term parking. The crowds parted for them. Well, not for him, for Niki. And, as he'd expected, she went straight to the driver's door, holding out her hand for the key. When he didn't hand it over right away she turned to him.

"I want to drive your new convertible. Top down, of course."

He used the button that popped the trunk and tossed the key to her as he stowed her carry-on luggage in a way that would let the trunk accept the top. His car was a three year old BMW hardtop convertible. Bright red, and perfect for Niki. Not what he would have chosen for himself, but what his father had decided a young up-and-coming attorney should drive. He'd handled a divorce for one of his dad's golfing buddies and this had been the payment his father negotiated for him. It was a great car, but Brad would have preferred something less ostentatious. The old Jeep he'd been driving since high school, for instance. The one his father insisted no one with any self-respect would be caught dead in.

The motor roared to life and the top began folding itself into the trunk before Brad could reach the passenger door.

"I love it," Niki said, but her grin faded as he crawled into the leather bucket seat beside her. "But you don't, do you? This is Daddy's idea, right?"

She whipped the Beemer out of the parking lot and had it up to fifty in the twenty-five-mile zone well before the red light at Valencia. "Well, at least he didn't insist on something dull."

Brad had to admit that. Given their father, it might have been some huge black limo, complete with pinstripes.

"I'm making myself live with it."

"But you've still got the Jeep, right?"

He smiled. "Don't tell Dad."

"Never." She got rubber in three gears as she headed north on Tucson Boulevard, past the ever-increasing sea of identical cracker-box houses, part of the mindless expansion that was Tucson's chief industry, even in the middle of the worst hard times most people could remember.

"So Daddy hasn't mellowed. Still telling you how to live your life and forcing awful things like this BMW on you," Niki teased. "And yet you're happy. You must have a girl."

Niki could read him like a book.

"Yeah, actually, I do. Or I hope so, anyway."

"Cool. Tell me. And has Daddy met her yet?"

"No." The grin left Brad's face. "Though she's supposed to come to dinner with us tonight. I'll need your support."

"You'll have it if she's good enough for you."

"Now you sound like Dad."

"I trust your judgment, big brother. But you know what they say—trust but verify. Tell me more. Who is she?"

"She's a cop," Brad said.

Niki whipped through the turn from Benson Highway onto Kino Parkway. "You're going to need more than my support. Senator Albert Ellis Cole's scion dating a cop? I hope she's made deputy chief at least."

"Not hardly," Brad admitted. "But she's an attorney, too. Passed the bar and everything. Just working in law enforcement instead."

"And you haven't told Dad the cop part, right? Well, at least there's room for a woman to advance in TPD or the sheriff's office these days. Which is it?"

"Sewa Tribal Police, actually."

"Sweet Jesus," Niki said. "Bradley Ellis Cole, if you bring some lowly Native American maiden into our father's house, even your baby sister won't be able to help. Not unless that sister is prepared to admit she's been dating a black guy. And she is certainly not prepared to do that. Besides, it wouldn't help. Daddy'd just put me straight into a convent while arranging your lobotomy."

◇◇◇

"Why are you in the office today?" the sheriff asked Mrs. Kraus. He had sent Mrs. Walker home in the "custody" of her attorney, arranged to have her car impounded, documented the crime scene with a couple of digital photos, and asked the congregation of witnesses to write up their testaments and leave them with their pastor. Then, rather than carry on a conversation about a murder threat in front of an audience, he'd gone to the courthouse to confront his office manager. The building was a block away, and he found it empty of creatures stirring, with the exception of Mrs. Kraus.

"I'm playing a computer game, if you must know."

Mrs. Kraus' face glowed as bright as Rudolph's nose with the admission. Her recent addiction to cyberspace gaming was not widely known.

"Surely not…"

"Well, sir, I got to admit it. That *War of Worldcraft* game really hooked me, even after…."

Some local kids had invented a computer game of their own with links to WOW. It had evolved to include real bombs, fixed elections, and a professional hit man. Mrs. Kraus had shocked him when he found she had become an aficionado of massive multiplayer online role-playing games—MMORPG to insiders like Mrs. Kraus. Or she had been until those kids started threatening her avatar with their online super demon.

"Got to admit I've missed it. I must have complained to your brother and his girlfriend. Anyway, I was opening my packages this morning when I discovered they sent me the latest upgrade."

Pam and Mad Dog had been playing WOW and gotten targeted by the same kids. As a direct result, Mad Dog's house had been blown off the face of the prairie by a rocket propelled grenade.

"I don't think Pam and Mad Dog are playing anymore." Mrs. Kraus said as the sheriff got a folder out of his drawer, wrote "Walker" on it, and stuck his notes inside. "But they told me to just transfer my character to a new realm and rename her. I shouldn't have any problem. Tens of millions of people play this game. What are the chances I'll run into wackos again? Anyway, I couldn't wait to try it. Which is why I was here when Don Crabtree called. Said he was going to murder one of the Conrad boys, soon as he figured out which one deserved it, unless you get right over there and arrest the pervert in question."

"And what did this pervert do?" the sheriff asked as he put the new folder in their file cabinet.

"Sacrilege. Foul, evil desecration of our Lord Jesus Christ."

The sheriff closed the drawer and raised an eyebrow.

"That's pretty near word for word what Crabtree claimed," Mrs. Kraus said.

"He get any more specific?"

"No, sir," Mrs. Kraus said. "I couldn't persuade him to explain. But I think you should go right over. By the time he hung up, Don Crabtree had about convinced himself it had to be Bub, the oldest Conrad boy. You know they're right across the street. And Don said something about taking a gun and...."

The sheriff missed what came after because he was out the door and halfway to his vehicle before she finished.

◇◇◇

Mad Dog staggered back across the living room and steadied himself against one of the loungers facing the TV. The severed hand couldn't be real. He looked down and noticed a drop of blood on his foot, an elegant argument for a different conclusion.

He felt an overwhelming sense of unreality, followed by a not-in-Kansas-anymore moment. What the hell were you supposed to do when someone hand-delivered a...?

Argh! That wasn't the way to phrase it.

He supposed the normal response to an unattached human hand showing up in the branches of your Christmas tree was to call 9-1-1. But Mad Dog had a thing about cops, even if his half-brother had been the sheriff of Benteen County, Kansas, for most of their adult lives.

When your physical appearance was so obviously Anglo and yet you'd legally changed your name to Mad Dog and proclaimed yourself a Cheyenne shaman, cops tended to look at you funny. And they tended to start thinking of you as the killer even if there were no bodies. This time they'd find part of one.

There were four cops in the whole world Mad Dog trusted. First, his baby brother, Englishman. Englishman because you had to have one of those when your last name was English and everyone had started calling your high school football-hero brother Mad Dog. But Mad Dog couldn't think of a good reason to contact Englishman. His brother was half a country away. And his sage advice would be to call 9-1-1.

Heather English, Englishman's daughter and Mad Dog's niece, was second on his list. She had the advantage of being nearby, a member of the Sewa Tribal Police. But she was working today. If he called, she'd have to treat it as official. Besides, she probably wouldn't have any more idea of what this might be about than Mad Dog did. She hadn't been in Arizona all that long and, from what she'd told him, wasn't exactly benefiting from chit-chat around the water cooler at headquarters. She had few meaningful contacts among the powers that be who might help him handle…er, cope with this bizarre situation.

Sergeant Parker of the Tucson Police Force's bomb squad had been a deputy for Englishman once. Mad Dog trusted her, and she'd been in this part of the country long enough that she might have some insights. But Three Points was in the county. Not her jurisdiction.

That left Captain Matus. The man had blamed a murder on Mad Dog right after Mad Dog arrived in Arizona. Someone who leaped to conclusions like that wouldn't normally have made Mad Dog's list, but Heather had persuaded the Captain to see the light and then Mad Dog and Matus had saved each other's lives while trying to bring a professional killer to justice. When it was over, Matus persuaded Heather to come work for him. And helped Pam find a job at the Sewa casino after she lost her Las Vegas piano-bar gig because she'd rushed to Tucson with some crazy idea about saving Mad Dog from the psycho murderer who was after him. Mad Dog realized how crazy it seemed for a beautiful girl to risk herself for him, but he wasn't about to walk away from luck like that.

No contest, Mad Dog decided. He found his cell and dialed Matus. Three Points wasn't in Matus' jurisdiction, either, but the man knew his way around county law enforcement. If anyone would help a Cheyenne shaman decide how to handle this, it was the Sewa warrior at whose side he'd fought once before.

"Matus," the captain answered.

"It's Mad Dog. I'm sorry to call on Christmas but I need a hand…Actually, I've got a hand. That is, an extra one. Not mine, you see. Unattached and….

"Shit," Matus said. "Why is it, if anybody else called and said something like that, I'd just think they'd misspoken? From you, I'm not even surprised."

◇◇◇

"Where are you?" Matus asked Heather.

She told him. She was only about a hundred yards up the trail from where she'd left her unit, an elderly Toyota Land Cruiser so scratched and dented that the Sewa Tribal Logo was almost unrecognizable. She'd had to hike that far to get enough bars on her cell.

"You're absolutely sure it's Hyde?"

Heather was, and told him why.

"Damn!" he said. His voice began breaking up but she understood the exclamation clearly enough. She continued downhill toward the Jeep. Maybe if she plugged the phone into the car she'd get a little more power and a better signal. Or she could use the radio.

"…can't wait. How soon…get to your uncle's place?"

What he said came to her like random pieces of a jigsaw puzzle. She tried to put it together but didn't like the way it fit. It sounded like the Captain wanted her to go to Uncle Mad Dog's. Why? The letter? But she couldn't. With the death of a well known politician like Joe Hyde, she needed to get back up that trail and make sure the crime scene remained secure until half the law enforcement personnel in Southern Arizona descended on the spot.

"What?" Heather said. "I couldn't understand."

The phone did Rice Krispy imitations in her ear and then reception was suddenly clear as a bell. "…so I'll come take Hyde, but you've got to get to Mad Dog's place as fast as you can."

"Why?" Her one word question demanded multiple answers. Why should she leave what was probably the highest-profile crime scene in southern Arizona since the OK Corral? What was going on at Mad Dog's?

"…called 9-1-1. Promised…sheriff's deputies. You know how Mad Dog is with cops. Get there quick."

And then his signal was gone. Completely, this time. No sound. No bars. Another dropped call. She still didn't understand. But apparently Captain Matus was coming here to cover the investigation of Hyde's hide. And, apparently, there was trouble at Mad Dog's. Something that required law enforcement—in this case, Pima County deputies. If she understood, the Captain had been on his way to help Mad Dog deal with that. Now, he felt he had to deal with Hyde's high-profile case.

Heather ran the last few yards to her unit. She considered the radio, then decided it might not be a good idea to broadcast any of this to the rest of the on-duty officers, to say nothing of people monitoring their channel. She plugged her cell in and tried Matus again. Nothing. She tried Mad Dog and didn't do any better.

She could wait here. The captain was on his way and could explain fully when they were face to face. But he'd said get to Mad Dog's as soon as possible, hadn't he? If that was the case and she didn't....

Heather remembered the last time Mad Dog got involved with police officers. Everything that could go wrong had gone wrong. Mad Dog ended up the target of a Tucson-wide search with orders to shoot him on sight.

Heather started the Land Cruiser, turned it around without adding new dents from a host of convenient boulders, and headed for Three Points. She probably could help her uncle. She was a cop and she had a law degree. She'd even passed the Arizona bar. If Mad Dog was in trouble, she could assert his right against self-incrimination and start pushing a judge to set bail. Not that Uncle Mad Dog was a criminal. But Joe Hyde had been flayed and Captain Matus would have to get that word to every relevant law enforcement agency in the state. And Mad Dog was mentioned in that letter. With her uncle's luck, the governor's car would turn up under Mad Dog's ramada and Mad Dog would be sitting on the porch reading a book about skinning animals for fun and profit.

Heather decided Captain Matus was right. She hurried.

◇◇◇

Don Crabtree hopped up and down in the empty Kansas street like a kindergartner in need of a potty break.

"Well, what are you going to do about this?" he said.

Crabtree lived on the north side of Buffalo Springs, his back yard ending in a wheat field. Like everyone in town, he made his living from farming and ranching. But after years of scraping by on half a section, he'd sold out and taken a job with the local co-op. It didn't pay big, but it paid steady. That made Crabtree more cash-rich than the average county resident.

When Crabtree moved to town, he bought a red-brick ranch-style at the edge of the city limits. It was a nice place, attractive from the street, except near Christmas time. Then the house disappeared behind Crabtree's passion—Christmas decorations. Santas, reindeer, elves, flashing light displays, toys, action figures, and his pride and joy, a life-size crèche. The Baby Jesus had been stolen nearly every year until Crabtree began chaining the infant to its cradle—not a customary way of depicting the arriving Prince of Peace. That was why the sheriff's first glance, after making sure Crabtree wasn't carrying a gun, was at the manger. Jesus in chains was right where he should be.

"Do about what?" the sheriff asked.

"Don't you see it? My God, man, right there."

And then the sheriff did see it. Yellow snow, just in front of Jesus' crib. The sheriff walked down the street to get a better angle.

"I want somebody hung up by the nuts for this."

"For what?" the sheriff said. "Pissing in the snow?"

Crabtree reached in his pocket. For a bad moment, the sheriff thought the man might pull a gun. He was that angry. What Crabtree filled his hand with, however, was a pair of glasses. He stuck them under the sheriff's nose.

"Are you blind. Look at it. Read what it says."

"Guess I am." The sheriff dug out his own glasses, the bifocals he tried to avoid wearing. When he put them on, the yellow pattern in the snow finally made sense. Someone, with a very full bladder, had let loose in front of Crabtree's Christmas crèche. That, by itself, would have been enough to heat the man's temper to broil. But the culprit hadn't been satisfied with such a simple sacrilege. He'd left a message in "flowing" script. The sheriff just managed to suppress a smile as he sounded it out.

"Gold, Frank n ¢, & Coors."

◇◇◇

"Nice doggy," the Pima County deputy told the hundred-pound silver wolf that stepped from behind a shaggy tamarisk to block his path to Mad Dog's porch.

"She's a hybrid and mostly wolf," Mad Dog said. "Not a dog."

The officer nodded but Mad Dog noticed the man drop his hand to the butt of his service weapon.

"She doesn't bite," Mad Dog said, "unless someone deserves it. You're perfectly safe."

"Good," the officer said. "But would you mind putting her on a leash or in a pen or otherwise securing her?"

"You ever try to put a leash on a wolf?" Mad Dog didn't address the other possibilities. He didn't have a leash or a pen. He'd never found a way of locking Hailey up anywhere she didn't want to stay. He shrugged. "I'm sorry. This is her yard. But she really is no danger to you. Unless you draw that gun."

Hailey ignored the conversation. After giving the deputy a thorough inspection from a respectful distance, she trotted to the porch, jumped up and put her feet on Mad Dog's shoulders. She slathered him with a kiss that wet him from chin to forehead, then dropped to lie at his feet where she could keep an eye on the nervous stranger.

Was this going to cause trouble? Mad Dog could see the officer considering his options. Hailey had all her shots and Mad Dog could prove it, but she wasn't wearing the required tag. She didn't do collars.

"How can we help you?" Mad Dog decided to just move past the issue. It wasn't like he didn't have a bigger problem waiting in his Christmas tree.

The officer came no closer and his hand stayed on his weapon, but he didn't argue about Hailey.

"I'm supposed to lend support to the Sewa Tribal Police. I was asked to meet Captain Matus at this address."

"Yeah," Mad Dog said. "I was hoping for that, too. But I guess he won't be here after all. Apparently something bigger came up."

"Yes," the officer nodded again. "I just heard. Is Matus sending someone else? Do you know why he wanted us to lend a hand?"

Mad Dog winced at the phrase. He chose to answer the first question instead of the second. "Sewa Officer Heather English should be here any minute."

"Good. But that thing that came up. It requires as much of our attention as possible. I can't hang around waiting. Do you know what Captain Matus needed?

"Well…." There didn't seem to be a way of putting this off. Mad Dog backed up to the door and opened it. Hailey got to her feet and went in. Mad Dog hoped she wouldn't chew on the evidence. "Maybe you should come inside."

The officer didn't move, obviously no more comfortable with the prospect of following a wolf into a house than Mad Dog was with trying to explain the severed hand in his living room.

Another car pulled into Mad Dog's yard. A silver Mercedes, trailing a cloud of dust. Until he realized it was a Mercedes, Mad Dog thought Heather might have arrived in the nick of time. She owned a silver Honda. Instead, the door opened and a spectacular woman got out. A rope of black hair was coiled at the back of her head. Obsidian eyes matched her conservatively cut suit and leather attaché case. Her face looked like it belonged on an Aztec goddess. She went straight to the deputy and handed him a card.

"Anjelica Grijalva," she announced, "of Castillo, Villareal, and Debowski."

An attorney. The law firm she represented meant nothing to Mad Dog, but it obviously impressed the deputy.

"I'm sorry, officer, but my client won't be answering any questions at this time."

◇◇◇

Since her father was a sheriff, Heather knew all the reasons she shouldn't use her cell phone as she drove to Mad Dog's. Englishman had told her and her sister often enough, citing statistics and even providing vivid descriptions of the bodies and cell phones he'd pried out of car wrecks. In one case, he'd found a cell phone literally inserted in the corpse's ear, all the way into the brain cavity.

It was good advice, but it didn't stop her. It wasn't every day you stumbled across a governor of Arizona, skinned and tacked to a wall. And then she'd gotten pulled off the crime scene of the century because her uncle had some kind of emergency. That Captain Matus had ordered her to leave the governor before anyone replaced her must mean Mad Dog had a real problem.

Once on the highway, Heather got bars back on her cell. She punched the button that auto-dialed Uncle Mad Dog's home number. No answer. When she tried his cell, it went straight to voice mail. That was so like him. Call for help, then not answer your phone. And not stay near it while you kept your cell turned off so whoever you'd asked for help wouldn't be able to get in touch with you. Argh!

Heather dropped her phone in her lap and just drove after that. She might have been able to get a decent connection with Captain Matus before he lost his signal as he climbed into those mountains, but that would mean both of them were driving too fast while using phones. Heather didn't want to put her boss at risk. And she didn't want him to know she was the type who dialed and drove at the same time, either. Not unless she had a clearly urgent situation that required it.

The doublewide Mad Dog and Pam had rented was on the south side of Three Points. The points were created by the junction of Arizona highways 86 and 286 at what was also known as Robles Junction. Ajo Way, aka 86, came out of the south part of Tucson on its way across the Tohono O'odham Reservation aiming toward the pleasures of Mexico's Sea of Cortez. Or to tiny desert outposts like Why, Arizona, or the turnoff to Kitt Peak with its crown of astronomy observatories. It was a sad highway, lined with broken bottles and flowered crosses.

Three Points was twenty-five miles southwest of downtown Tucson. Highway 286 began or ended there. Its ribbon of asphalt ran south to the border crossing at the village of Sasabe. Ran beside the Sewa Reservation, too, recognizable because of its Flowers of Gold Casino. Heather made good time. Route 286 was never heavily traveled. On Christmas Day it was practically deserted.

Mad Dog's place stood beside a dirt road, just beyond several other manufactured homes in varying stages of disrepair. The one custom-built Santa Fe-style monster in their midst might have been worth a fortune in a more consistent neighborhood. Heather crossed a dry wash filled with brush and mesquite that masked the view of Mad Dog's yard until you were right on top of it. The yard was empty. So was the carport. No surprise. Pam would have taken the Mini Cooper to work. Heather pulled up in front of the house and got out of her Sewa tribal Land Cruiser. It wore a fresh coat of rusty brown dust from the back roads she'd just driven.

There was no sign of Mad Dog. Not even when she called his name. The front door was open. That might have worried her, but Mad Dog didn't believe locked doors prevented burglaries. Heather ran up the steps, crossed the porch, and rapped on the door's knocker before going in.

"Uncle Mad Dog? It's me."

A breeze whispered through the bougainvillea beside the trailer's west wall. A cardinal answered from the mesquite bosque along the wash. No response came from the house except a faint clicking. She pushed the door wider. Hailey, thick in her shaggy winter coat, ran to greet Heather from where the wolf had been examining ornaments on the Christmas tree. Her claws ticked on the linoleum floor and she wagged her tail in enthusiastic welcome. Heather bent and hugged the wolf and then realized what Hailey had been inspecting wasn't an ornament. As soon as she understood what she was looking at, Heather went over and confirmed that the amputated hand still had its skin. It did. That meant she might be dealing with her second murder of the day. And it meant Uncle Mad Dog could be in very big trouble.

◇◇◇

Edna Crabtree looked like she could lift the corner of a John Deere and hold it in case someone needed to swap out a tire. What she held, just then, was a hefty mug of coffee for the sheriff. English took it, waved off the cream and sugar, and nodded his thanks.

"I told Don not to bother you on Christmas Day, Sheriff. But you know my husband and his yard decorations." She turned to her husband and shook her head. "Don, I wish you'd calm yourself and let this go. Allow our sheriff to enjoy his holiday."

The look on Edna's face was like that of a young mother whose child had just done something naughty but adorable. Don Crabtree paid her no attention. He'd snatched up his own mug and begun pacing back and forth across the kitchen floor like a soldier guarding the oven. Considering the delicious aroma of roasting turkey issuing from there, and the microwave meal the sheriff could look forward to once he got home, Crabtree's blocking access to the bird might be wise.

"This is serious." Crabtree did an about-face at the refrigerator. "I mean, it's not just the personal insult of someone doing their business in our yard. It's the sacrilege to our Lord Jesus. I'm thinking this SOB could be looking at real jail time."

The sheriff nodded, and not just to placate Crabtree. If he found the guilty party, and Crabtree pressed charges, a Benteen County judge and jury might just take the insult to Baby Jesus as seriously as Crabtree had.

"Mrs. Kraus said you suspect the Conrads across the street?"

Crabtree nodded. "Those boys have always been wild. And everybody knows they drink. Besides, when I was out there photographing the evidence this morning, I saw them staring out the window laughing at me."

"Now Don," Edna pleaded. "You got to admit, but for the sacrilege part, some people might find this funny."

"I don't got to admit no such thing, Edna. I can't imagine anyone finding the tiniest bit of humor in such a despicable act."

The sheriff was glad he'd suppressed his own smile. "Sorry, Don," he said, "but I've got to agree with Edna. I know several people who will laugh out loud when they hear about this. Your evidence against the Conrads is pretty shaky, but I'll have a word with them."

Crabtree sputtered, but he didn't say anything, or go get a gun to take care of the neighbors on his own.

"When did you first notice the, uh, evidence?"

"First thing this morning."

"He's like a little kid about that stuff," Edna said. "Just can't get enough of looking at it. Shuffled out there in his slippers before coming to bed last night, then risked frostbite again the minute he woke up. And nothing between him and a terrible chill but his PJs and robe."

Crabtree shot his wife a dirty look. "And a good thing I keep an eye on it, too, the way this turned out."

"So it was fine last night?" English asked.

"It was."

"And the damage had been done when you got up this morning?"

"The blasphemy was right where you saw it, plain as day."

"When was that?" the sheriff asked. "And when did you go to bed?"

"Daddy always goes to bed right after the news—10:30 on the dot."

The sheriff had been watching Crabtree pace and hadn't noticed their teenage daughter enter the kitchen. She wore bunny slippers that made no sounds on the tiles. Her hair was disheveled and her face was creased with pillow lines. That and the oversized sweatshirt she apparently used as a nightie convinced English she'd just gotten up. The kitchen clock read just short of one. The girl was pretty and built too well for greeting visitors in such skimpy attire. But she didn't seem aware of it as she skirted her father to help herself to a cup of coffee.

"About time you were up," Crabtree growled. "When'd you get in?"

"I don't know," she muttered.

"Just after three," Edna said, the cheer drained from her voice.

"Was my crèche all right then?" her father asked. The sheriff thought Crabtree might pick up on his daughter's late hours and address them, once he got past what had happened in his yard. Or after Edna had a word with him. "Did you notice? Had somebody urinated in our yard?"

The girl's face was looking away from the sheriff. The chrome finish on the refrigerator showed the blurred reflection of what looked like a grin cross her face.

"What are you talking about?" she said as she turned to her father. No grin. Just a cute and confused little-girl look.

"If you didn't see anything," Crabtree said, "the sacrilege must have occurred between three and five. That narrows it down."

"Daddy, are you saying Baby Jesus got peed on?" No doubt, now—smile a mile wide. "Oh my," she laughed. "Somebody's gone and paved their road to hell with yellow snow."

◇◇◇

"You picked a good place to hide," the attorney told Mad Dog, "but you should have let your people know where you were."

Mad Dog didn't say anything because he didn't know what she was talking about. He hadn't been hiding and he didn't have people. In fact, he didn't know why he'd gotten in the Mercedes with her.

"Or maybe not," she continued. "Hard to know who to trust right now. But they found you. We know they discovered your location. That deputy might have been working for them. You're lucky I got there when I did."

The deputy had been seriously pissed. In fact, Mad Dog thought he might get arrested for…well, he wasn't sure for what, or even if the deputy needed a reason. That was part of why Mad

Dog got in Anjelica Grijalva's car when she told him to. Also, because she obviously expected to be obeyed—no arguments. Hailey hadn't stopped him. She just curled up in front of the door so the officer would think twice about searching the premises.

"Do you know why the deputy was there?"

Finally, something Mad Dog could respond to. "The hand," he said. "I'm guessing he was there about the hand, though he didn't act like he knew about it."

Grijalva took her eyes off the road for a moment to give him a searching glance.

"Hand?"

"The one that got left on my front porch this morning."

She looked at him again.

"In a box. By a brown truck. I thought it was UPS."

"A hand. A human hand?"

"Yeah. With a big gold signet ring engraved with a snake that had feathers."

"Your people told us Quetz has gone missing," she said.

It took a minute, but the name finally registered. Quetz—it could be short for Quetzalcoatl. That was the name of the Aztec god whose human form was fair-skinned. Hernán Cortéz had conquered an empire because of that coincidence.

"Your people don't know what Quetz may have told the opposition. If they took him alive. But this is a good sign. They sent you his hand as a message. They could have just sent an assassin. Maybe they want to talk. To bargain. I wonder why."

So did Mad Dog. Along with why sending a hand as a message was a good sign. And who she thought Mad Dog was. He was having second thoughts about accepting this ride.

"Uh, where we going?"

"Your people suggested the warehouse. The armory is there. And enough of your soldiers to hold off an assault."

"Armory?" Mad Dog said. "No." He was increasingly sure he shouldn't have gotten in the car. Guns? Soldiers? She must think he was some kind of crime boss or revolutionary or...

well, he didn't know what. But she definitely had him confused with someone else.

"No?" she said. "Maybe you're right. They could take that as a sign you plan to strike back. Maybe we should stick to your strategy of laying low and staying out of sight. But you have to talk to your people. And your enemies. See what they want. We could go to my office. No one will be there today. Or my place. I'm sure you know, *Rabioso*, you're paying me enough to provide you with anything you want."

Mad Dog turned and gave her a closer look. She was a very beautiful young woman. For a moment, he envied this *Rabioso* guy. Then Mad Dog remembered the hand and his foolish flights of sexual fantasy were replaced by another wave of nausea.

◇◇◇

The professional killed for pay and for pleasure. Plenty of pay, this time. He expected to net over twenty mil. And things were going well. He was nearly finished with his contracts. Before the day was out, he would pause to take his pleasure. All work and no play made Jack a dull ripper, he thought, and let himself smile.

The décor inside the Nogales whorehouse improved as you rose above the service floors and entered the realm of management. Bawdy gaudy gave way to dark wood, thick carpets, and leather furniture. The professional noted the change and was neither surprised nor impressed. He'd been searched just inside the street entrance. They took a gun and two knives from him. That left him with three deadly weapons secreted on his person, so he was singularly unimpressed with Cowboy's security. Still, two very large, very muscular men escorted him upstairs to the carved doors that apparently led to Cowboy's office. They spoke softly into an audio-visual device beside the entrance and, a moment later, the doors opened.

"Who's this queer?" a young man across the desk from Cowboy asked in Spanish.

The professional and alleged queer didn't react. The man who'd spoken was tall with ropy muscles and a scar that turned his expression into a perpetual sneer. He didn't think the professional spoke Spanish. Or didn't care.

It would have been an insult in English. Not just politically incorrect. In this man's street Spanish, it was probably the worst slur he could imagine.

The two bouncers from downstairs led the professional into the office and stopped in front of the desk.

"Leave us." Cowboy was thick and muscular and aging. He sat behind the desk with his intricately stitched boots propped on its surface and a Stetson pulled low over bushy gray eyebrows. The younger man pushed himself off the edge of Cowboy's desk as the doors swung shut behind the bouncers. This guy was probably Cowboy's head of security. Unless Cowboy was fool enough to think he could take care of himself.

"Hey, little faggot," the man with the scar said, "you here to pick our new wallpaper?"

The professional smiled at scar face and cocked his head, as if he hadn't understood.

Cowboy shook his head. "Leave it alone, Nardo," he said. "We got a truce with Mouse. I promised to cooperate with his man."

Nardo sighed. "Up to you, Cowboy, but don't turn your back on him." Nardo did just that and wiggled his buttocks.

The professional raised an eyebrow and, addressed Cowboy in perfect Castilian. "With your permission?"

Cowboy scowled but nodded. "Sure," he said. "Within reason."

Nardo froze in mid-wiggle. Something very sharp slit through his trousers and tickled his nether regions.

"You see, Nardo," Cowboy said, "he speaks Spanish. And he may be small, but Mouse wouldn't send me a killer who's not good at it. You should learn to watch your mouth and not make assumptions."

"My back was turned," Nardo whined. But he didn't make things worse by trying to extricate himself from the situation.

The professional withdrew the blade and wiped it on Nardo's shirt. "Perhaps you are a man whose back should always be turned."

Nardo stepped away, gaining a little distance. "Who the fuck is this guy?"

"This is Mr. Smith. He's a messenger from Mouse. And Mouse tells me he's the man who can take *Rabioso* down."

Nardo hadn't learned yet. "You expect me to take shit like that from Mouse's Sodomite?"

Cowboy shrugged under his Stetson. "You'll take what I tell you."

Nardo spat on the carpet, took a step away, and then whirled on Smith with a knife of his own. "How you like it now, faggot? I'll shove some cold steel up your ass for what you did to me."

The professional, currently known as Mr. Smith, had sheathed his own blade. He didn't move except to smile, eyes on Nardo's weapon.

"Nardo! No!" For the first time there was real concern in Cowboy's voice. It caught Nardo off guard and his eyes flicked toward the desk.

That's when Smith took Nardo's knife, grabbed him by the hair, pulled back, and stretched Nardo's neck across a knee, throat up. Nardo's blade pressed tight against his own flesh beneath the Adam's apple.

"If this man is your bodyguard, he's worthless," Smith said. "You want to keep him?"

Cowboy took his feet off the desk and leaned forward. He pushed the Stetson higher on his forehead. "He is worthless and I should consider your offer, but he is my son, not my bodyguard."

"I see." Smith dropped the boy and the knife and withdrew his knee so fast Nardo's head bounced off the floor. "Then I won't kill him. And I'll only cripple him a little if he troubles me again."

"Holy Mary!" Nardo said. "Who are you, really?"

"Tell him," Cowboy said. It wasn't an order. It was permission.

"I am the deadliest assassin you'll ever meet. I'm so good, Mouse and Cowboy will pay me one million dollars apiece for killing *Rabioso*. While they are allies, I won't kill you. But give me another excuse, Nardo, and I will take great pleasure in hurting you. For the moment, I am Mr. Smith, but you, I think, should call me sir. Do you understand?"

Nardo looked in the professional's eyes and believed him. "Yes, sir."

◇◇◇

Heather knew she couldn't reach Captain Matus by phone, but she thought Sewa headquarters would be in radio contact with him. She called. They weren't. Under the circumstances, that meant no one was available to help her deal with an off-reservation problem.

As suggested, Heather next called the Pima County Sheriff's Office to report what she'd found. They weren't interested. They told her they'd send a unit when they could spare one. Her status as a Sewa tribal police officer didn't impress them. Especially since they'd already answered a call to assist a Sewa officer at the address she specified. No Sewa officer had been there, and the deputy who responded had labeled the incident a false report. That put her on their don't-hold-your-breath priority status. The next deputy to come to Mad Dog's would likely arrive only after the last treed cat in the county had been rescued.

Heather didn't like it, but she understood. They were understaffed, underfunded, it was Christmas, and they had another body part, a celebrity's, to command their attention. She was on her own.

Heather hung up and looked at the hand beneath Mad Dog's Christmas tree. Even Hailey had abandoned her while Heather tried to explain the situation to the Pima County sheriff's dispatcher.

She opened her cell phone again and selected the camera mode to begin documenting her second crime scene of the day. To be on the safe side, since she was in a location with decent cell service, she forwarded all her photos to her email. Then she went to work on the hand and the box it had come in.

With no other law enforcement agency prepared to help or take her seriously, she went into Mad Dog's kitchen after she finished with the pictures. There were a number of things that should be done and for the most part, she didn't think she could do them. But there was only one way to find out.

Heather considered the meat thermometer briefly. A human fever thermometer would be better, but she knew Mad Dog didn't have one. Mad Dog thought there was no point in knowing stuff like that because of the years he'd spent with a deductible on his health insurance that was so high the policy only kicked a few days after you became comatose.

If Heather could establish the hand's temperature, she might make it easier for the experts to determine how long it had been detached. Problem was, the indicator on the thermometer only began registering at 120°. As she held it by the probe, the red indicator moved. Not much, but she could mark it with her sharpie.

She also found a re-sealable plastic storage bag. That was good since she'd used her meager allotment of evidence bags on the governor's case. And, of course, she found the usual collection of utensils, dishes, cups, and glasses. Not much that was useful.

The meat thermometer didn't budge when she held it against the hand. Room temperature, she guessed. She briefly considered inserting the thermometer into the wound where once an arm had been attached, then decided against it. Puncturing the hand wouldn't do it any further damage, but who knew what forensic evidence she might disturb. She went back into the kitchen and thoroughly washed her hands, then returned and touched the back of the hand midway between knuckles and wrist with her own hand inside one of those storage bags. Its skin was noticeably cooler than her own. She knelt and sniffed it. No hint of meat gone bad yet. She dabbed the wound with her bagged fingers and found the blood drying, but still faintly tacky.

Without ever coming into direct contact with the evidence, she turned a plastic bag inside out and used it to pick up the hand, then reversed the plastic until she could seal the bag and take a really close look. There was nothing remarkable about the palm except a little section of unnaturally colored skin just above the wound. Part of a tattoo, she thought. If so, this end had been green. That was the extent of what she could tell about the image portrayed there. The hand was large, calloused enough to indicate the owner had used it for more than typing, though hardly shovel work. Nothing unusual about the back of the hand, either. The fingernails were short and clean and unremarkable, except the edge of the thumbnail was broken and jagged. Someone else's DNA might be under what remained of it. Or might not.

That left the ring. Using another, smaller, plastic bag, she tested it to see if the ring would come off without damaging the surrounding flesh. To her surprise, it did, easily. As she hoped, there was an inscription inside. Nothing personal, just COLORS – TUCSON. She had heard of the place—biker accessories located on Speedway. Not much, but maybe a place to start.

◇◇◇

"Sorry to interrupt your Christmas dinner," the sheriff said. Just over Roy Conrad's shoulder he could see a dozen people crowded around a dining room table piled with food. The Conrad boys, Crabtree's prime suspects, were among them.

"No problem, Sheriff. Always room for one more." Conrad's big smile, red cheeks, and plentiful belly gave him a slight resemblance to a cleanly shaven Santa.

"Thanks, no. I wouldn't bother you but…"

Conrad's face spread into an even broader grin. "It's about Crabtree's front yard, isn't it? Oh, Lord! That's hilarious. Couldn't happen to a nicer guy."

The sheriff had a hard time controlling his own grin. "Problem is, he thinks one of your boys did it."

Conrad's grin faded. "Why that son of a…chicken herder."

"So I hate to, but I have to ask…."

Conrad turned to the dining room. "Any of you go across the street and piss that message on Crabtree's yard?" he yelled.

He got a chorus of feminine giggles and masculine "no's" in reply.

"If I'd thought of it, I might have done it myself," Conrad said. "You got any idea what a pain it is living across the street from the perpetual Christmas fairy? 'Bout a zillion kilowatts of light pour through our front windows. Even heavy curtains can't darken a room. And the traffic it brings to the neighborhood. Folks pull off and block our driveway while they take it all in."

"Yes, sir. I wish I had the staff to send someone to help control that traffic."

"Not blaming you, Sheriff. I know how strapped the county is." Conrad sighed. "But I'm strapped, too. It hurts, when I struggle to pay our utilities with the thermostat set on sixty, to see all that conspicuous waste across the street. Look, I don't know how any of us can prove ourselves innocent. But the boys were both home all night and in their beds when I looked about four. Something roused me. Maybe some left over childish excitement for Christmas morning. Couldn't go back to sleep. Came down to the living room and opened my curtains. Got blinded for my trouble. But Crabtree's snow wasn't pristine then. Nobody came or went from this house last night before Crabtree started howling bloody murder about dawn. I give you my word on that, Sheriff."

"That's good enough for me," English said.

Conrad finished the thought for him. "But probably not for the ignorant elf across the street."

◇◇◇

Anjelica Grijalva lived on the southeast side of downtown near the railroad tracks. Her townhouse was on the third level of a converted warehouse. There was an elevator but Mad Dog preferred the stairs and Grijalva's well-turned calves and stylish heels had no trouble with them.

Each unit's front door opened off a balcony and used a coded keypad. A wide entry led into a wider still living area featuring a glass and leather décor with Southwestern touches, especially in the art hanging from rustic red-brick walls. Kitchen, living, dining, and office space were combined, with only folding screens to separate one area from another. The wall that faced the tracks was solid glass ribbed with steel supports. A glass door opened onto a terrace where gentle wisps of steam rose from the edges of a hot tub's cover. A profusion of potted plants surrounded it and gave it a jungle-like feel.

"The plants give me privacy," she said. "But there's a nice view of the mountains from the loft." She gestured toward a stairway that circled up to what must be her bedroom. "Want to check out the scenery?" She raised an eyebrow and Mad Dog indicated he'd take her word for it.

She pointed out a bathroom, offered him her computer or phone or a drink. When he declined them all, she told him to make himself comfortable. She'd give him some privacy to begin making his necessary contacts. And, with that, she disappeared up the curving stair, leaving him a departing smile, a wave, and an offer. "If you need anything, let me know."

Mad Dog needed advice. He activated his cell and tried Captain Matus. No answer. He called the Sewa Tribal Police and asked if the Captain was in. The Captain wasn't. He considered Heather and decided he was way too far out of her jurisdiction, especially since she was on duty. He considered Pam, but the whole situation had turned into something he didn't want to explain on the phone. Especially the part about being in the Tucson home of the extraordinarily attractive Anjelica Grijalva. That left him short on options. There were some Indian shamans he'd gotten to know. That Tucson cop. A couple of friends. He hated to bother any of them on Christmas, especially when he didn't know what he might be getting them involved in.

Pacing didn't help. Nor did staring out the wall of glass. He stepped away from it to pace some more and found Ms. Grijalva just behind him. She wore one of those terrycloth robes Mad Dog imagined the finest hotels provided their guests. It covered her pretty thoroughly, but clung in a way that hinted the only thing underneath was her. Mad Dog had to force himself to look her in the eyes.

"I should leave," he said.

"You're safe here. I was assigned to pick you up today because neither Cowboy nor Mouse knows anything about me. So you should stay. I thought I'd go relax in the hot tub. Wouldn't you like to join me?"

At least one part of Mad Dog's anatomy wanted to join her very much, but he didn't think Pam would approve.

"Nah," he stuttered, "thanks. I really should go."

"But I haven't offered you anything to eat." She reached down and opened her robe. Mad Dog couldn't help but notice that Anjelica Grijalva shaved her legs all the way up. And then some.

"See anything you like?" Her hands touched the front of his jeans. "Or maybe you'd rather be the first course."

◇◇◇

Even as Heather drove into the lot behind Kino Hospital, she was still trying to convince herself she'd made the right choice.

Heather had a problem. Several problems, actually. She desperately wanted to get back to the first crime scene and take part in the investigation into the new governor's death. That could be a career-maker. But she was stuck in the middle of the bizarre situation she'd found at Uncle Mad Dog's—that was no partridge in his tree. And Uncle Mad Dog, who had apparently called for help with the problem, had gone missing. That left her in possession of a severed human hand in need of an intact chain of custody, putting it, ultimately, in the hands, no pun intended, of the Pima County Medical Examiner's Office.

Turning it over to PCME would normally have been a matter of course. Criminal investigators from the Pima County Sheriff's Office, who had jurisdiction in unincorporated Three Points, would have contacted someone from the office. A medico-legal death investigator would have been dispatched, or at least a contract employee authorized to transport human remains. But Heather couldn't get a deputy back to Mad Dog's house. And, while she was a law enforcement officer in Pima County, Mad Dog's place certainly wasn't in her jurisdiction. If she called PCME for a pickup, she wasn't sure they'd send someone. On Christmas Day, they'd be short of personnel. And, if the PCME's office contacted the sheriff's department, they might not bother at all. Not after they learned the sheriff's office was treating this as a false report. So Heather had finally convinced herself she had to deliver the hand personally.

One option had been to take the hand to Sewa Tribal Police Headquarters. That was south, more or less back toward the governor's death investigation—a case she should be deeply involved in by sheer right of discovery. Or she could take it to the Pima County Sheriff's Department, where she was likely to get held up for hours, maybe even turned into a suspect. Her last option was the medical examiner's office to just hand it over. Argh! She couldn't even think about this without tossing off morbid puns.

Well, she'd made her decision. Since Sewa Tribal Police still couldn't put her in touch with Captain Matus for advice, she'd headed for PCME. She pulled into the medical examiner's parking lot behind Kino Hospital. There would be someone here to take delivery, even though they might not be happy about the circumstances. Still, they'd take it, even on Christmas. Death, violent or natural, never took a holiday. The ME's office was always staffed. And then she'd go to Colors. That was where the ring the hand had been wearing came from. The business would normally be closed for Christmas, but she'd seen a story on the news last night. Tucson's biker community—the ones who drove chopped Harleys and wore club leathers—was throwing a Christmas party for homeless children and their families in Colors' parking lot today. Mesquite grilled turkey was being served and stuffed toys handed out to kids. Someone from the business was bound to be there. Someone, she hoped, who could tell her about the ring.

Hell, Uncle Mad Dog might even be there. Why not? He had to be somewhere. That somewhere probably had something to do with what she was about to hand off....

Argh!

◇◇◇

What most bothered Sheriff English, as he made his way across the street to Crabtree's glowing Jesus-in-Toyland exhibit, was the shotgun he'd noticed propped near Conrad's door. The man was a pretty stable fellow, but apparently he felt threatened. He might not have said so to the sheriff, but that gun was a pretty clear indication he felt his sons' lives were at risk. This little cold war could turn hot and deadly all too easily, and the sheriff wasn't sure what to do about it. If he had a competent deputy to park in the street and keep things quiet until the case was solved or tempers cooled…. He didn't, though, and despite the season, wishing would not make it so.

Crabtree opened his front door before the sheriff could knock. "You make an arrest?"

"No. I didn't. Roy Conrad gave me his word his boys had nothing to do with it and I believe him."

Crabtree made a disparaging noise but the sheriff stayed on message.

"If you want me to find out who urinated in your yard, you've got to promise me you'll stay in this house and not so much as stare out the window toward the Conrads' place. Can you do that for me?"

"This is my property," Crabtree said. "I will not be told how to behave on it or whether or not I can look out my own windows. If I feel the inclination, I'll arm myself and go out there and march a perimeter to prevent further assaults on my land and my God."

"Now, Don, calm yourself." Mrs. Crabtree came up behind her husband and put a restraining hand on his shoulder.

He shrugged it off. "Edna, get me a gun out of the study." He pulled a heavy jacket off the hall tree beside the front door. "I'm going to set up surveillance by the crèche right now. Let them Conrad boys know their lives will be on the line if they come back over here."

"Well, Don," the sheriff said, "since you've threatened to kill one, I'm going to have to arrest you if you step outside with a gun."

Edna and Don did double takes worthy of a sitcom. And Don began yelling threats while Edna began shouting, too. In her case, pleas for the sheriff not to arrest Don, and for her husband to quiet down and not get himself in real trouble. At least neither of them went to get the aforementioned gun and the sheriff didn't have to draw his.

The sheriff spent several minutes trying to get a word in edgewise. Crabtree's threats and attitude made it impossible for him to leave the man armed and marching around his yard while Conrads with guns considered how to protect themselves. The county's Christmas task force, Sheriff English, would have to stay there and keep them apart instead of going in search of someone with an especially large bladder capacity.

Sheriff English didn't think Crabtree was the type to start shooting, either at the sheriff or the Conrads, but if the man began an armed patrol of his decorations, Conrad was likely to march out the front door with his own weapon. An exchange of pleasantries might well lead to an exchange of lead. Trouble was, the sheriff also couldn't imagine Don Crabtree, now apoplectic with rage, coming peaceably. Given the sheriff's limited recovery from a bullet to the spine a few years ago, he wasn't sure he had the strength to get his cuffs on Crabtree. By this time, the man had convinced himself he was the misunderstood and mistreated victim, about to be humiliated in his own home.

The sheriff could call for back up, but his only deputy was the sort who brought gasoline to throw on fires. The sheriff decided he'd have to settle for sitting guard duty in his vehicle to keep the men apart. Until spring maybe, or until he froze solid inside the old Taurus. But before he could beat a strategic retreat, the Crabtree's daughter elbowed her way between her parents, pushed open the door, and offered the sheriff a long cardboard box.

"Here are all Daddy's guns," she said. Her parents went suddenly silent with shock. "This being Christmas, maybe you can leave him here and take his guns instead. That way he's no threat to the Conrads or anyone else. Mom and I'll see to it he doesn't run over there with a carving knife. Won't that work?"

"All of them?" Crabtree said. He seemed a little concerned about that.

"Even the little derringer that fits in that fancy belt buckle," she said. "How about it, Sheriff?"

"Yeah," he said. "That'll work." He accepted the box and was surprised at how much it weighed.

"You can't take my guns," Crabtree whined. "It's unconstitutional."

"I'm not seizing them," the sheriff said. "I'm just taking them into safe custody for the moment. Soon as this is cleared up, you can have them back."

"Thank you, Sheriff," Edna said. "I'm just as glad to have them out of the house."

"What about my Second Amendment rights?"

"It's Christmas, Daddy. There aren't any militia gatherings today."

The sheriff looked the girl in the eyes, answered her smile with a small one of his own and a nod of thanks. He started for the street.

"Uh, Sheriff," Crabtree called after him. "That Uzi. The man who sold it to me guaranteed it's legal. Assured me you can't set it to fully automatic anymore."

The sheriff loaded the box into the back of his station wagon and turned around to face the house. "I'll check that out for you. Best find your paperwork on that purchase, though. Just in case."

The sheriff climbed behind the wheel, started the Taurus, and pulled into the street. He could see the butt end of Don Crabtree's pickup in the driveway behind him. There was a bumper sticker on it suggesting Don's hands were now cold and dead. If the Uzi was automatic, the sheriff thought, Don had cause for them to be at least cold and clammy.

◇◇◇

This situation, or variations on it, had been the stuff of Mad Dog's teenage fantasies from the moment he learned oral sex was not just the product of his perverted imagination. And then, during his commune summer, he'd learned to give and receive it as nothing more than a casual kindness. But that was then and this was now. He and Pam had a commitment. STDs were lots more common and more deadly than when he was young. He no longer believed he was immortal. And besides, Ms. Grijalva scared him.

She popped the first button of his jeans expertly, he noted, before he took a step back and began defending his right to say no.

"Uh, thanks," he said. "I give at home."

She looked up at him and smiled. "Would you like some Viagra first?"

"No, really. Got someplace I need to be." He looked at his Casio, failed to register the time, but managed to say, "Wow. That late already."

Mad Dog buttoned his pants, stepped around her, being careful to remain just beyond her reach, and sprinted for the door. He grabbed his jacket and took the steps down to the parking lot two at a time, then hit warp speed on his way toward the street. He looked over his shoulder, fearful she might be about to run him down and have her way with him out here in traffic. He needn't have worried. No traffic, and she stood on the balcony, wind opening her robe exposing the delights he'd declined to sample.

"Come back," she called. "You're safe here. Even from me, if that's what you want."

The sun broke though the clouds for a moment, highlighting her perfect body. It was as if he was being given one last reminder of what could be his if he'd just go back and let her nibble his apple. It was tempting, enough so that Mad Dog had to make himself face the street again and remind himself how much he loved…ah, Pam. Yeah, Pam.

Grijalva could get her keys and the Mercedes and be after him in a minute. He wasn't sure how many times he could say no. He cut left at the first cross street, dodged between a couple of houses, and set a healthy clip down a deserted alley.

Mad Dog pulled out his cell phone, turned it on again, and wondered who to call. He had some messages, but he wasn't going to stop running until he found a place to hide or felt safe or just couldn't keep going. Which, considering his pace, might not be long at all.

The girl was spectacular. Mad Dog couldn't remember ever having said no when a similarly willing temptation offered itself. Pam owed him one, he thought, and then decided that was an opinion he'd best keep to himself. In fact, if the segment of his anatomy—the one trying to persuade him one quickie wouldn't really count—ever rose in memory of the fabulous Ms. Grijalva, so be it. He'd share the occasion with Pam, but not the cause.

A pair of dogs followed him behind a chain link fence and sang Christmas carols. He realized they were the first thing he'd heard since Grijalva called after him. Other than his strained breathing. No people, no traffic, nothing but a few tall buildings to remind him he was in the heart of a city of a million people. He slowed and tried to catch his breath. Somehow he'd punched a number. His cell phone had called someone. That person was saying "Hello."

"Hi," Mad Dog managed to pant.

"Who is this?" the voice demanded.

That was exactly what Mad Dog wanted to know, too.

◇◇◇

The professional and Nardo crossed the border in Nogales using the DeConcini checkpoint. There were no problems. The professional's paperwork was in order, and he had left most of his lethal weapons in Mexico. It would take a very thorough search to discover the others.

Cowboy's son, Nardo, had brought plenty of weaponry. He'd stored it in a variety of compartments someone had neatly fitted in the Buick he drove. The professional thought Nardo wanted to use one or more of them to repay the humiliation he'd suffered in his father's office. But, if the young man had revenge in mind, he disguised it well. Nardo was on his best behavior. The boy got a little uppity with the border guards who recognized and deferred to him. The professional knew a lot of money had paved their way into the United States.

Christmas Day—fewer crossers than usual. People were already with their families, their holiday shopping complete.

After clearing the border, Nardo drove to a parking lot behind the McDonald's on Crawford. The spot wasn't visible from the checkpoint. Nardo nodded toward a Chrysler 300 on the far side of the lot, nearly alone in a place that was usually jammed full of cars.

"That will be Palmer," he said. "Mouse's man. Our contact."

"Yes," the professional said. "I know."

As the professional turned his head toward the Chrysler, Nardo reached into one of the Buick's disguised compartments. The professional hadn't moved his eyes when he moved his head. Nardo was a kid, impatient, picking the wrong time for his revenge. The professional's hand snapped across the Buick like a whip and struck Nardo in the throat.

"I told you I'd hurt you if you troubled me again."

Nardo made a noise. His hand came out of the compartment with a gun but the professional had no trouble taking it away. Nardo didn't really want it anymore. Instead, he clawed at his throat because his larynx was crushed and he couldn't breathe.

"I said I wouldn't kill you. Just hurt you. Does it hurt, Nardo?"

Nardo made the sound again. His neck bled, though not from the professional's blow. Nardo's nails tore his own flesh in his frenzy to get air. And his eyes stared, wide, fear in them. Begging.

"I could save you now," the professional said. "Open a hole in your trachea below where I hit you. If I do that, you'll be able to breathe again."

Nardo took his hands away from his bloody neck. He folded them together as if in prayer. He stared at the professional, pleading for his life.

"Oops! I'm afraid I've changed my mind. I guess I lied when I said I'd only hurt you. I've decided to let you die."

Nardo grabbed for the professional, but there was no strength in his grip anymore. The professional avoided Nardo's hands, watching the life slip out of the boy's eyes. Avoiding the blood, the professional opened the door and stepped out of the Buick. He pulled Nardo so the body lay across the console, invisible through the windows unless someone walked up to the car and looked inside. Even then, with the tinting, it would be hard to tell that Nardo was dead instead of just sleeping off a drunk.

The driver's door on the Chrysler opened and a middle-aged man, thick in his shoulders and gut, got out. Thick under his left arm, too, from the pistol he carried. He looked at the professional and nodded. "I'm Palmer," he said, stepping around the car to open the other door for the professional. "Welcome to the United States, Mr. Smith. Mouse sends his regards."

The professional shook Palmer's hand, and sat in the offered seat.

"What about the Cowboy's man?" Palmer asked. "I thought he was coming with us."

"Change of plans," the professional said. "He'll wait here in case anyone follows us."

"Not necessary," Palmer said. "But Mouse says you're the boss. So, if that's the way you want it?"

"It is."

Palmer had aimed the Chrysler out of the lot and turned toward I-19 by the time the professional asked, "Any word on *Rabioso*?"

"Which one? I hear the fruitcakes put the fake *Rabioso* in a velvet cage," Palmer said, a smile in his voice. "The other thinks he's disappeared. Mouse will tell you."

And that was the end of their conversation. The car ate up the empty road, passing atypical markers indicating the narrowing distance to Tucson in kilometers instead of miles, and the increasing distance from Nardo's corpse.

◇◇◇

Tradition in Brad Cole's family held that Niki, the baby of the family, got to put the first ornament on the tree every year. Until now, Niki had lived at home, so the Coles' tree was always up and resplendent at least a week before Christmas. Brad couldn't remember waiting this late. When he suggested putting it up before Niki arrived home, his father shot the idea down. Niki was the senator's little girl. Nothing as special as tree decoration could take place without her. Brad had wondered aloud whether they would have a tree at all if Niki had put off her first college holiday visit until New Year's Day. That got Brad one of those looks that made him think the senator could still write his son out of his will.

Brad and his father had an awkward relationship. For example, Brad didn't think the senator thing was the big deal his father made of it. Albert Ellis Cole had just been re-elected to his second term—state, not federal. And he hadn't emerged as a leader. The senator had voted for guns and against taxes and immigrants, but he'd refused to support Arizona's birther bill requiring the President to prove his citizenship before appearing on another Arizona ballot. Brad was proud of his dad for standing up against that one. He liked to think his father might still turn into a moderate. The senator had even explained on the senate floor that the United States President could not logically be both a Communist and a Fascist at the same time. But that was one of the few things Brad and his father agreed on, so talking politics was something they avoided.

Niki was delighted to be the reason they'd waited to put up the tree. But after two strings of lights and half-a-dozen ornaments, she wanted to start opening presents and eating turkey. Mom grumbled, but Dad gave in immediately. Whatever the senator's little girl wanted. Brad could have been jealous, but he'd never been able to do anything other than adore Niki.

Niki gave her parents a pair of Cornell sweatshirts. Brad gave them books. His mother liked chick lit and cozy mysteries. His dad, political thrillers with a conservative bent. Niki got perfume, a cashmere sweater, jewelry, and an envelope. "A little treat for our favorite student," the senator said. Inside it were reservations and brochures for a summer tour of Europe. Brad was impressed. His own gifts included a couple of dress shirts, some ties he'd never wear, and a small square box the senator handed him without comment. It contained a Rolex.

"Thanks," Brad said, trying to make himself sound as enthusiastic as Niki had been about her gifts. Niki shot him a sidelong glance and a raised eyebrow, but then the phone rang and she grabbed it.

"Merry Christmas," she said. "You don't have to bring me a present. Cash would be fine." Then the grin slipped from her face and she handed the phone to her father. "I don't think the sheriff will bring me cash," she said. "He wants to talk to 'The Senator'—and right now."

The senator gave his daughter a big smile as he accepted the phone, then said, "Maybe I should take this in my office."

"I'll go see if the turkey's ready," their mother said.

"What's with the watch?" Niki asked. "I mean, I know it's expensive, but it doesn't hold a candle to what they gave me and, besides, it's boring."

"It's a message," Brad told her. "They gave me one just like it for my birthday, but I haven't worn it. You know how I feel about ostentatious stuff like that."

"And Daddy doesn't?"

"Oh, he knows," Brad said. "But he thinks I need to flaunt it to get my career headed in the right direction. This is his way of forcing the issue. Sort of a 'wear it or else' message."

"Will you?"

Brad unbuckled his Timex and stuck it in a pocket. He slipped the Rolex on his wrist and winked. "Sure, today anyway. Don't want to piss the senator off when I'm bringing a new girl over for his approval tonight."

The door to the senator's office opened. He stepped out, pale. Every ounce of Christmas joy had drained from his face.

"Daddy, what's wrong?" Niki said.

"Governor Hyde has been assassinated," the senator said. "I've got to…. I need to…."

But the truth was, Brad knew, there was not one thing the senator had to do. Or could do, even. He was important enough to be informed, but not important enough to be involved. He wasn't in the line of succession. The legislature was in recess. The senator was just as helpless under the circumstances as any other citizen. And that, Brad understood, more than the fate of the governor-elect, was what had taken every breath of wind out of the senator's sails.

◇◇◇

Sheriff English stored Crabtree's arsenal in the jail at the back of the Benteen County courthouse. He secured the guns in an eight-by-eight cell with the aid of a chain and a padlock. Most of the cells' keys had gotten lost over the years. But that didn't matter because nearly all the locks were rusted open or closed and the upper levels weren't safe anymore. The roof had leaked back here for most of the century the building had stood.

The sheriff put off testing the Uzi, or any of the rest of the guns. Right now, he needed to find out who'd urinated on Crabtree's crèche. Otherwise, sooner or later, Crabtree and Conrad were going to have a confrontation and, short of sitting on one or the other, there was no way the sheriff could prevent it. But where to start?

Crabtree's high wattage decorations invited pranks. That was why Crabtree had chained Jesus in place. The sheriff supposed he could eliminate half the county's residents because they lacked the appropriate plumbing required to leave a message in that particular manner. Otherwise, nearly every male in the county was under suspicion. Except the Conrad boys. The sheriff had looked in Roy Conrad's eyes and believed him.

With no immediate idea on where to begin his investigation, short of going back over to Crabtree's neighborhood and knocking on every door, he stepped into his office. Mrs. Kraus was at her computer, slaughtering hordes of enraged pansies. Lavender, white, yellow, blue—it didn't matter. She was making them bleed. Her fingers flew on one side of the keyboard and her right hand skittered about directing the mouse, clicking little rows of colorful squares that seemed to cause her on-screen character to throw thunder bolts and flames and strange bursts of light into the advancing floral assault. The pansies dropped charred petals in their tracks. It was like watching a really high-quality animated feature film, the sheriff decided, except Mrs. Kraus wasn't just watching, she was part of it.

He cleared his throat.

"A minute," she said. "Gotta do some pruning."

"Okay," the sheriff said, "but...."

"Shhh! Gotta concentrate."

Something fat and fluffy slipped in and out of visibility at the corner of Mrs. Kraus' screen. While it was there, it was teddy-bear cute, except for the expression on its face and the pair of intricate swords in its cute little paws.

"What about...." the sheriff began, but Mrs. Kraus shook her head and made an angry noise as she laid into the pansies again.

The last one fell, spilling chlorophyll into the soil at Mrs. Kraus' avatar's feet. "There," she said, and began to swivel her chair to face the sheriff.

"Uh," the sheriff began. But whatever he'd been about to say was drowned out by the shrieking attack of the bladed bear.

Mrs. Kraus swung back to the computer, stabbed a key, but not before the bear stabbed her avatar. Repeatedly. Mrs. Kraus' avatar, which the sheriff had noticed was unusually young and trim and attractive, resembling its owner only in hair color, slumped to the earth as the teddy bear laughed and began dancing on Mrs. Kraus' corpse.

"Damn," she said. "Ganked my toon again."

The sheriff decided not to ask what that meant. "I don't supposed anyone else has called to complain about having holiday decorations vandalized?"

"Jeez, it's just a wimpy level seventy-three Wereteddy, too. Wait till I catch up with that fuzzy bastard."

"Ah..., complaints?" the sheriff reminded her.

"No, no complaints," Mrs. Kraus said. "But one of the members of the church brought over the witness statements you asked for. I filed them. And he said something about the holidays being stressful and all. Mentioned something about hearing the Porters had some lights shot out on that American flag decoration they put up this year."

"The Porters? Dave and Marian?"

"Yeah, six miles east and two south of the blacktop. Quiet sorts who keep to themselves and don't bother anybody. Then somebody shoots their flag. That seems kind of over the top."

The sheriff agreed.

Mrs. Kraus turned back to her computer and said, "You got to excuse me now. I need to rip the heart out of that teddy bear and make him eat it."

◇◇◇

A big guy stepped out of the crowd in front of Colors and approached Heather's Toyota the moment she pulled up. He was exactly what you'd expect of a bandit biker—muscled arms bulging out of a sleeveless leather vest, tats, chromed chain belt. And hanging from that belt, a holstered pistol. Heather dropped her hand and unsnapped the strap that kept her SIG Sauer in place before she stepped out of the vehicle to meet him.

The big guy nodded. The heavy chrome rings in his ears made his lobes wobble. He smiled, displaying a gold incisor. "How can I help you, officer?"

She hadn't exactly expected friendly from this crowd, but then she hadn't expected to run into an armed guard before she even got out of her truck.

"I'm looking for the owner or the manager of this business."

He surprised her and offered her his gun hand. "That'd be me. They call me Doc, though the name on my business license is Joseph Wall."

His hand enveloped hers, but his grip was firm, not crushing.

"Heather English," she said, "Sewa Tribal Police. You mind if I ask why they call you Doc?"

"Ph.D. in astronomy. Bikes are a hobby that kind of got out of hand. Oh, and what's in this holster is a radar gun. Choppers that come in here, if they're speeding, I raise my prices. It's kind of a gimmick, but I'm trying to get our customers to change their image. I'm not trying to persuade bikers to change the way we look, but I hope to demonstrate to the general public that we abide by the law, same as everyone else. So, tell me, we got some kind of problem with the Sewa Nation?"

"Uh, no." Heather felt embarrassed by the unsnapped strap on her SIG, now that she could see Doc's holster didn't contain a firearm. "I wanted to ask you about a ring you made here."

"Make lots of rings. If it's one of the skull and crossbones or the mock SS death's heads, doubt if I can help you much. They're too popular."

"No. This one's different." Heather pulled out her cell phone, called up her pictures, and showed him a shot of the feathered-serpent ring, one she'd taken when it was off the severed hand.

"Quetzalcoatl, the plumed serpent. Aztec's patron god of knowledge. Yeah, I remember it. That was a one-off. I thought we did a nice job on it."

"Can you tell me who bought it?"

"Sure. Mousy little guy. Elvis Presley, he called himself. Couldn't have looked less like the King if he tried. Wanna see the paperwork?"

Doc led her across the crowded parking lot, past people feasting on heaping plates of turkey and fixings, past kids hugging new toys, past a black-leather-jacketed guy in a Santa cap, passing out brightly wrapped boxes.

"You have an address?"

"No. That I remember. This Elvis is a little guy. Kind of skittish. Balding. Carrying concealed, too, if that's of interest. Of course that's legal now. I've got a phone number for him, but he never gave me an address. I didn't care because he paid cash in advance."

Doc opened Colors' front door and held it for her.

"You say he was little? This ring, it's big. Would fit a guy with big hands, maybe as big as yours."

"Not quite that big." Doc flashed the gold tooth and showed her the way to his office. "But you're right. Would have almost made a bracelet for Elvis. I figured maybe Elvis has a boyfriend." Doc thumbed through a file cabinet. "Elvis Presley, here he is." He handed her the order.

The ring had been expensive and a rush job. Just a month ago. The phone number looked like a cell.

Doc headed for the front door. "I hear some choppers coming. I wanna catch them if they're speeding. Call him from here if you want. Leave the paperwork on my desk when you're done. Then come join us for turkey."

"Thanks, Doc," Heather said.

The door closed behind him and she pulled out her own cell and punched in the number. She expected it to go unanswered. Or to learn the number was no longer in service. Instead, a man's voice, high and nasal said, "Blue." The word was clear enough, and though Blue was not exactly a standard greeting, it certainly brought a response to mind.

"Suede Shoes," Heather said, prompted by the Elvis reference.

"Check. That you, Angel?" the voice asked. "You find that Dog guy again?"

Heather only knew one Dog guy—her uncle. Angel, she didn't know, but she doubted she could pass herself off as Angel very long. What answer did he want? What answer might get her more information? She took a guess. "Yes," she said, keeping her voice soft.

"I got it. You're whispering, don't want him to hear. You back at your place?"

"No," Heather said, and took a chance. "Where you want him?"

"Your place. Like we planned. Keep him occupied till Smith wants him."

"He won't go there," Heather tried, hoping.

"Well, shit. Then take him to the armory."

Armory? Who the hell had an armory, Heather wondered.
"No. Not there either."

"Well, ain't that fine and dandy. Where, then?"

"You want him," Heather said, "you take him."

The voice went quiet for a minute, then turned smarmy.
"You'll owe me."

"Sure," Heather agreed.

"Big time. Know what I mean?"

"Sure," Heather said again.

"Then bring him. Remember how to get here?"

Are you kidding? Heather thought. She didn't let the jubila-
tion reach her voice, though, when she said, "No."

"First right south of the swap meet. Right again. First lot
past the one with the boats. You can start thanking me when
you get here."

Heather scribbled in her notebook like crazy. "Whatever you
want." She whispered to Elvis, who giggled a little hysterically
before hanging up.

Half way back to her truck, Doc offered her a platter heaped
with holiday fare.

"Can't," she said. "Got a date with Elvis in the jungle room."

◇◇◇

"End your call, Mr. Dog."
Mad Dog had thought he was alone in the alley. When he
turned, he found a young man wearing camouflage a few steps
behind him. And the young man pointed a weapon at him. Or
was it a weapon? It looked like a toy shotgun complete with a
bright yellow butt and grip.

"What?" Mad Dog said, totally confused by how the man
seemed to have come out of nowhere and how he knew Mad
Dog's name and, for that matter, who he'd accidentally called
on his phone.

"I said who is this?" the someone on his phone answered.
"Your voice sounds like a Cheyenne shaman I got to know in
Kansas. Is that you, Mad Dog?"

"The phone," the young man reminded him, looking simultaneously serious and silly in his starched uniform with a beret cocked jauntily over his eyes.

"How'd you know my name?" Mad Dog said.

"Oh come on," the phone said. "You called me. Is this some kind of practical joke or did you hit my number by mistake?"

Mad Dog recognized the voice on his phone. Considering how his afternoon was going, Sergeant Parker of the Tucson Police Department was probably exactly who he'd most like to talk to just now. Only there was this kid with his uniform and toy gun.

"Your name was included in my field briefing," the kid said. "Now end that call and drop the phone. You are my prisoner and I require your immediate compliance."

"Mad Dog," Parker said. "What's going on there? Did I hear someone call you their prisoner? Where are you?"

Mad Dog thought he might be able to stall the kid and maybe get some help from Parker if he worked this right. "Did you follow me from Anjelica Grijalva's apartment to this alley…" Mad Dog glanced at the mountains and added, "…maybe six blocks West of the railroad tracks?"

"Of course," the toy soldier said. "But the phone…you've really got to obey me about that. If you don't…." His eyes dipped toward his gun for a moment.

"Oh, come on," Mad Dog said. "That's not a real gun. That's some kind of toy."

"Can you see a street sign, Mad Dog?" Parker whispered. "Are you near some unusual building that might help me find you?"

"Toy?" The boy's cheeks suddenly sported two bright red spots. "I assure you, Soldiers of the Free State Militia are not issued toys. I could kill you a hundred times over with my regular weapon, but I've been ordered to take you alive. That's why I'm carrying this, instead."

"So it isn't a real gun," Mad Dog said. "I didn't think so, not with those yellow bits that are an even brighter shade than that two-story Victorian house behind you. The one with the Santa mannequin on the balcony."

"I know that place," Parker said. "I'll be right there, but be careful. There are some strange weapons on the street these days."

"You're trying to tell the person on that phone where you are," the kid said, his voice suddenly outraged at Mad Dog's failure to respect his authority. "You, sir, are about to discover exactly what kind of gun my Mossberg X12 LLS is."

"The Mossberg, that's a Taser shotgun," Parker said. "It's for real. A non-lethal stun gun, unless you're too close. Then the projectile it fires can kill you as dead as any bullet."

Mad Dog had been tasered before. He had no desire to repeat the experience. And the kid was less than ten feet from him.

"Ok," Mad Dog said. "Here's the phone."

He tossed it, and as he'd hoped, the kid let go of the gun with one hand to pick the phone out of the air. Mad Dog broke for the closest fence. He jumped, caught the top rail, pulled himself up. And then something popped and his brain shut down.

◇◇◇

Palmer and the professional pulled off Stone and into a parking space behind a radio and television repair facility that looked like it had been deserted since the CD era began. A weathered FOR SALE sign out front reinforced that interpretation, its contact information hidden beneath several layers of graffiti. A couple of other cars occupied the lot—a middle-aged Ford pickup and a nondescript Chevrolet sedan at least half-a-dozen years old. The lot was screened from the street by a six-foot concrete-block wall and an abundance of oleanders that had been getting more attention than the building's exterior. The businesses on either side appeared abandoned.

The professional let himself out of the Chrysler and offered Palmer a compliment. "Not what I expected."

"Pays to keep a low profile. Let's go in. Best not to stay in one place too long, even a place like this."

That was true. The professional didn't expect to be here long. Just long enough to finish his business with Mouse.

Palmer pushed a button beside the back door and waited. He waved at the roof. "It'll be a minute. They'll check us out with the cameras first."

The professional couldn't see the cameras and wondered if they were really there. Probably.

The door opened and a man who looked a lot like Palmer stepped out and checked the two of them and the parking lot, then stood aside so they could enter. The man was carrying in a shoulder rig under his right arm—left-handed. The three of them stepped into a small room and waited while the second goon secured the door behind them.

"You want to pat me down?" the professional asked.

"If it was up to me," the guy said. "But Mouse says no."

"Sign of trust," Palmer said, though the professional had noticed the metal detectors built into the back door's frame. His weapons weren't metal.

Another door opened. A third man, this one dressed in blue jeans and boots and a leather jacket waited within. The next room took up most of the building. At the far end, stacks of boxes and bales of product were neatly lined against a wall. Much nearer, across from the door they entered, was an old desk. It held a computer monitor, a keyboard, a printer, a phone, and the buttocks of a small man with a rat-like face and mousey brown hair. The little guy wore an impeccably cut suit, expensive shoes, and a red power tie held in place by a Mickey Mouse tie tack. He stood, all five feet of him, including the platform heels, and advanced with his hand outstretched.

"Mr. Smith. It's a pleasure to finally meet you in person." He took the professional's hand and shook it—didn't hold on too long, or squeeze too tight. Firm, manly, but not welcoming. Mouse needed the professional. That didn't mean Mouse liked it.

"What's the situation?" the professional asked. "Do you have what I asked for? And are the principals where they're supposed to be?"

"Straight to business, no chatter," Mouse said. "I like that in a hired killer."

"I prefer the term professional assassin."

Mouse backed up and hoisted himself onto the desk again, his feet well off the floor. "Yes," he said, though it was clear he didn't see the distinction. He waved at the man in the jeans and leather jacket. "This is Bill. He's part of the package you asked for. The rest is in that truck out back.

"Bill, you won't mind stepping outside and waiting for Mr. Smith, will you? It's to your advantage not to hear what we're about to discuss."

Bill didn't say a word. He left the room, escorted by the left-handed gun. Mouse leaned back and looked at the computer monitor and the professional decided there must really be cameras covering the parking lot.

After a moment, Lefty returned and Mouse faced the professional again. He recited an address. "That's where our competitor, Mr. *Rabioso*, is holed up. Can you remember that?"

The professional nodded. He already knew. Besides, he had perfect recall. He remembered everything, including the pleasure he'd taken from watching the life go out of Nardo's eyes in that Nogales parking lot. Almost as satisfying as watching the same thing happen to the first man he killed when he was twelve.

First boy he killed, really. Seventeen, eighteen maybe. And big. A bully. The professional had a name then, though he'd had so many since it no longer meant more than the others. He'd been clumsy and slow the first time. But his piano-wire garrote bit into the victim's neck, cut through skin and flesh and the boy couldn't get hold of the wire while the professional slowly tightened it. The bully took a long time to die. Using the garrote and tightening the wire had been agonizing because of the burns on the professional's hands—where his mother had decided to put out her cigarettes the night before. The professional liked remembering the look on the bully's face. Liked reliving every moment of every kill.

"Hey," Mouse said. "You still with us?"

The professional was surprised. He'd let his attention slip. That was not acceptable.

"Yes," the professional said. "Go ahead."

"It's a safe house. *Rabioso* thinks we won't find him there. He has four men with him. Some others come and go. I don't know exactly how many are in the house at the moment. You wanted him to feel safe so I've kept a loose watch on him." Mouse shook his head. "This part seems foolish to me. I have enough men to go in and take him out. Especially if Cowboy and his people help. It would be messy but certain. How will you do it alone?"

"I won't be messy," the professional said. "Besides, you and Cowboy are turning on *Rabioso* to steal his territory. Do you trust Cowboy not to do the same to you? Do you want Cowboy to know when the real *Rabioso* goes down?"

Mouse rubbed his chin. "I hope you're right," the little man said, "and that you're as good as you claim."

"Watch and see," the professional said. "Now, what about the others?"

"We set up our false *Rabioso*. The Grijalva girl lost him. I understand they killed her for that. But they've reacquired him. No problem there. And Cowboy's people took the bait. They're maintaining loose surveillance on that *Rabioso* the way we are on the real one. Using this false *Rabioso* brought that girl you wanted off the reservation. She's trying to find him like you said she would. And I've got a man following her for you. She went to a biker place on Speedway a few minutes ago. You mind telling me how she fits in?"

"She's not directly related," the professional said. "She's part of what you're paying me." In fact, she was the reason the professional had taken this job. She lived here, and he had unfinished business with her. He'd faced her before and she'd beaten him. No one else had ever done that, except his mother, who'd inconveniently stepped in front of a speeding truck before the professional got around to repaying her for nurturing him through childhood. Heather English excited him. She was worthy. Or nearly so. He would face her again. He would fight her. He would finish her this time. And if he made millions on the rest of this, that was just icing on the corpse.

"And I'm paying you a hell of a lot of money," Mouse said. "I don't care about the girl. Just curious. The way I'm curious to know how you managed to get all of Southern Arizona's law enforcement tied up on that reservation. The new governor, that's the rumor I'm hearing. Is that possible?"

"Where I'm concerned," the professional said, "anything is possible."

Mouse shook his head. "Then I am impressed. If you can take *Rabioso* fast enough, the extra million I'm paying you to betray Cowboy will be worth it. My people will control *Rabioso's* operation and cripple Cowboy's before nightfall. Talk about a Christmas present."

The professional didn't say anything. He watched Mouse.

"Do you need anything else?" Mouse asked, growing uncomfortable under a stare that never seemed to blink.

"No," the professional said. "I think I have everything I need to insure satisfaction."

Mouse got off the desk and offered his hand again. "I like that too—satisfaction guaranteed, and before final payment."

"Yes," the professional agreed. "But sometimes satisfaction is more important than payment."

"What?" Mouse looked confused as the professional slammed his palm into Mouse's face, driving the little man's nasal cartilage into his brain and killing him instantly. The professional pivoted and kicked the left-handed thug in the crotch before the man began to react to what had happened to his boss. The professional planted a palm strike into Palmer's sternum almost simultaneously, interrupting his attempt to pull his gun. Both men collapsed, temporarily unable to defend themselves. The professional would have enjoyed taking time to finish them in some creative fashion, but he had another use for them. He pulled a small plastic syringe from its hiding place in his sports coat and injected each with a drug that would keep them unconscious for hours.

Bill was waiting out back in the old Ford's cab. The professional handed him a map and an address.

"Go there," the professional told him. "Knock on the door. You're expected. Then wait for me. Don't speed, but don't waste time. Mouse hasn't got all day."

In fact, the professional thought, Mouse didn't have more of this day, let alone any future ones.

◇◇◇

Sheriff English hadn't driven by the Porter place in ages. He was surprised at how dramatically it had changed. Fresh earth had been graded up to the edge of the ditch so that none of the yard could be seen from the road. Just the second story of the house showed, and all the windows up there were shuttered closed. There was no hint of the allegedly damaged decoration—lights in the colors and shape of an American Flag. The only flag stood atop a pole and flew, the sheriff was shocked to see, upside down.

Political protesters had been known to fly American Flags upside down. Dave and Marian Porter weren't the type. In fact, the sheriff had heard they were pretty conservative. That left the sheriff considering whether they might be flying an upside-down flag for its original purpose—a distress signal.

The sheriff turned into the drive, which now curved through the new berm on the other side of the ditch. It brought him to a steel gate that could be pulled aside, though not without effort, on wheels mounted along its base. The sign, KEEP OUT – THIS MEANS YOU, further confused him. This was Benteen County. Friends and neighbors and even occasional lost strangers in search of directions were always welcome. But apparently not by the Porters.

The sheriff shut off the Taurus and climbed out. He still couldn't see most of the yard or any part of the lower floor of the house from the gate. He pushed his hat back and considered what to do. With his bum leg, he'd play hell climbing that embankment.

"State your name and business." The voice was tinny and hard to understand and it took the sheriff a moment to discover it came from a speaker on a post beside the gate. There appeared to be a microphone beside it. The sheriff bent and spoke into it.

"Is that you, Dave?"

"Who wants to know?"

"Why, it's me, Dave," the sheriff said, and then realized Dave and Marian Porter didn't really know him well enough for that to be sufficient. "Sheriff English," he added.

The Porters were quiet folks. He'd see them doing their shopping in town occasionally. They'd always taken the time to speak politely for a moment, the sheriff inquiring about Marian's family—Dave had none surviving, and they had no children of their own—and how Porter's crops were doing. The Porters, in turn, would ask after the sheriff's daughters or suggest he seemed to be getting around better and that they were pleased to see it. Then both parties would go their separate ways.

"You aren't welcome here. Not if you've come to disarm us. You should know we are prepared to defend our rights. We will not give up our guns." And then Dave Porter read the sheriff the Second Amendment to the Constitution of the United States.

"A well regulated Militia, being necessary to the security of a free State, the right of the people to keep and bear Arms, shall not be infringed."

After that, the only sound was a faint hiss from the cheap speaker and the wind sweeping through Porter's trees. This being Central Kansas, where the wind always blew, it sounded like silence.

What the hell was going on here? He'd come to ask about a rumored assault on a flag decoration and was being met with a recently fortified farm yard and the broad hint he might be shot if he were to trespass on their property.

"Why on earth would you think I've come to take your guns?"

"Because I've heard the Obama confiscation has begun, and that you, as a representative of our new totalitarian government, are going about the county seizing arms."

"Have you been talking to Don Crabtree?"

"I will not reveal my sources to the representative of a tyrannical regime."

"Dave, somebody urinated on Don's yard this morning. A bad joke is all I think it was. But Don decided the Conrad boys did it and threatened to kill them. I was about to arrest Don, until his daughter gave me his guns and begged me to let her and her mother keep him for the holiday. That what you're talking about?"

"That's not the way I heard it."

The sheriff shook his head. "No, I don't suppose it is. But if I were out running around the county seizing guns on the order of the federal government, do you suppose I'd be doing it by myself? Check the sky, Dave. There aren't any helicopters up there, black or any other color. It's just me out here in my old station wagon, sitting at your gate."

The sheriff looked at the berm again. The earth, where the most recent snow hadn't stuck, was quite fresh. Surely not, he thought, but he couldn't help from asking. "This gate and your earthworks, you didn't throw these all up for me, did you?"

Dave Porter read him the Second Amendment again, then added, "But no, I graded and built that gate earlier this week. Installed the speaker yesterday."

"For God's sake, Dave, were you expecting me to come seize your guns, then?"

"I been expecting someone to come try and take my guns since this Marxist-Fascist government seized power. But I hear you're well-armed for the task now. That you've got automatic weapons with you. All of Crabtree's weapons, for that matter. That gives me pause, Sheriff."

So that Uzi was an illegal weapon. The sheriff decided he would give Don Crabtree reason to regret its purchase. Less for having it than for spreading wild rumors.

"I'm carrying that same old .38 Smith and Wesson I've had for years. Nothing else. If I've got automatic weapons, they're Crabtree's, and they're locked in a jail cell back in Buffalo Springs.

I'm not here to take your weapons, Dave. I came because I heard someone shot out some lights on a decoration you put up and I thought it might be the same person who caused this morning's troubles. If I can determine who that is, I might be able to keep the Conrads and the Crabtrees from killing each other. That's why I'm here. Though I decided I should inquire about your upside down flag, as well."

The silence returned for a few moments, and then Dave Porter stepped around his earthworks, threw his shotgun to his shoulder, and fired. The sheriff almost fell on his butt from surprise. Trying to jump to a shooter's stance so he could draw his gun and defend himself proved more than his bad leg would allow and he ended up leaning against the side of his Taurus.

"Damn coyote running down the middle of the road, bold as brass," Porter explained. "And I clean missed him."

The sheriff finished checking himself for fresh wounds. Besides the shotgun, he noticed, Porter had a pair of pistols strapped to his waist. At least he wasn't pointing anything at the sheriff.

"Jesus, Dave. I thought you'd killed me."

The man had the good sense to look embarrassed. "Well, I apologize. For the less than gracious greeting, too, especially on the day of our Lord's birth. But until I reassure myself, I'm not letting you in."

"You don't have to. But can you tell me, please, if someone shot at some decorations you put up?"

"They did. Five nights ago. Put out a bunch of bulbs in the Old Glory display I hung up on our front porch."

"Were you or Marian hurt? Those bullets, did they penetrate your house? Are they embedded somewhere I might recover them? They could point me to the culprit. And, once I've found him, I'll convict him."

Porter looked down at his boots and scuffed the dirty snow with one. "Well, they weren't bullets, exactly."

"But you said…?"

"Rocks. Smooth river pebbles. From a slingshot if I had to guess."

The sheriff spread his arms, taking in Porter and his guns and gate and earthworks. "And so you...."

"Well," Porter confessed, "I may have overreacted a little."

◇◇◇

Sergeant Parker wouldn't normally have spent Christmas at Tucson Police Headquarters, but that's where she was when Mad Dog called. In the usual scheme of things it would have taken a bomb to get her there on Christmas Day. That was because she was the star of TPD's bomb squad.

This Christmas was different. She, like virtually every off-duty officer in Southern Arizona who'd heard, had headed for the office to be useful or hang around and wait for news. It was a catastrophic day for law enforcement when an Arizona governor-elect got himself assassinated, especially in such a spectacular fashion.

At least the media didn't have the story yet. Or the few reporters who'd heard hints had been persuaded to sit on them.

When Mad Dog's call went dead, Parker slapped a Post-It with her cell number on the entrance to her cubicle and ran out. She grabbed a bomb squad buddy, jumped in her personal car, a Ford Focus, and pointed it west. They were only a few blocks from the gentrified part of residential downtown where that yellow Victorian house stood. She could drive there faster than she could get a unit to respond on a crazy day like this.

"Where we going?" Anderson asked. Anderson was a compact little man who thought fast and moved slow—unless the situation required otherwise. A good combination when your job obliged you to handle materials that could leave nothing behind but bone shards and tooth fragments to put inside your flag-draped coffin.

"A friend of mine's in trouble." Parker knew Mad Dog and his brother thanks to the events that ended her first stint with TPD. A routine traffic stop turned into a domestic situation on steroids. A man had rigged a bomb to his wife. It killed her. So Parker ran away and took the law enforcement job least likely to put her in a similar situation. She became one of Englishman's deputies in Benteen County, Kansas. Just in time, of course, for a series of bombings. She'd saved some lives, regained her confidence, and turned herself into the person you wanted around when an explosive device turned up.

Sergeant Parker knew a bunch of stories about Mad Dog and his wonder wolf. She began lining up the best ones for Anderson, after she told him what this was all about. But Anderson's mind was elsewhere.

"Are they positive that skin was the new governor's?"

"That's what I hear." It was a subject she wanted information on, too, but she had to get Anderson ready for the situation they faced. "We're looking for a big guy—six-two, bulky, shaved head. He was threatened by someone with one of those Mossberg Taser shotguns. You know what they look like?"

"Sure, like a toy."

"If I got the address right, it's going to be somewhere around Railroad and 15th. In view of a yellow Victorian with a Santa Claus on the balcony."

On any day but Christmas, Sergeant Parker couldn't have crossed downtown Tucson in a hurry without lights and siren. But the streets were as empty as she had ever seen them. The houses were probably packed—people opening presents and sitting down to holiday feasts. A few new bicycles wobbled down the streets, but no cars. And, when they got there, she found no sign of Mad Dog or his assailant. Parker cruised around the block. Then another.

"What I heard," Anderson said, "was Governor Hyde came down to go hiking with his daughter. Now he's flayed and she's missing."

"You sure, or is the missing daughter a rumor?" Parker turned another corner. Kids played football in a yard and a UPS truck crossed the street a couple of blocks down. Nothing else.

"Hell," Anderson said. "Nobody's saying anything officially, but I heard about the daughter from a Captain who ought to know."

Hyde chose a trophy wife for his second marriage. His first wife had given him a daughter who should be about eleven or twelve now. That wife lived up in Oro Valley—a long way from the Sewa Reservation where Heather English, Mad Dog's niece of all people, had apparently found the governor's skin. The connection between Heather and Mad Dog was one reason Parker had taken his wild phone call seriously.

"Don't see how they can keep this thing quiet much longer," Anderson said.

Parker agreed. She was on the verge of deciding this was another wild Mad Dog chase and returning to headquarters. She circled around to the original location she'd thought Mad Dog might be calling from for one last look.

Then she saw the cell phone at the foot of a fence. This was a paved alley. It bordered on back yard fences and the fronts of guest houses and garages. In the midst of a financial crisis that had struck local government about as subtly as an atomic weapon, the paving here was strewn with pot holes. The edges of the alley were difficult to define, but the phone was a little too geometrical and a little too shiny to blend with broken asphalt.

"What?" Anderson said as she slammed on the brakes and piled out of the car. She pulled a plastic glove out of her pocket, picked the phone up, and checked the last number called—hers.

"Your friend's?" Anderson was right behind her, hand on his service weapon, surveying the alley and the yards beyond.

"And possible evidence of a kidnapping," Parker said, "that might be related to the governor's case."

"You're shitting me," Anderson said.

She didn't explain. Something she'd just seen didn't make sense.

"Say?" Parker said. "Does UPS deliver on Christmas?"

◇◇◇

Heather wished she had time to dress more appropriately for Elvis and the jungle room—anything but her tribal uniform. Wished she could exchange her marked Sewa patrol unit for something that didn't shout cop. But a delay could spoil this. Even the time it would take to check in with tribal authorities and explain where she was. Besides, they'd probably tell her to get the hell back to the reservation.

For now, they were busy with the governor. That was clear from the radio chatter. Though the chatter took care never to mention their VIP corpse. They were trying to keep this from making the news as long as they could. So, once she got Elvis' address, Heather simply switched her radio off. Left her cell on—set to vibrate, which seemed appropriate for the jungle room. Captain Matus and the tribal police still had a way to contact her, but she could decide whether to answer.

The place turned out to be a junkyard. And not a well-organized one. There wasn't any sign to indicate a business name or sales office. The yard was filled with old cars and abandoned appliances. No collector's items, and no people. She cruised slowly past and pulled around a fence leaving her four-wheel-drive out of view from the lot. She stayed behind the fence, as best she could, and approached the yard's battered chain link gate. It hung crooked and open. The only structure on the property was a trailer—old and tired, its once jaunty-pink siding now sunburned and peeling, its tires flat and rotting to shreds.

A stack of concrete blocks stood in front of the trailer's door. Heather avoided them, moving to the side from which the doors opened—out for a screen door that would no longer stop flies smaller than a microwave, in for a main door that looked to have been kicked in more than once. She listened for a moment. Music. Blue Hawaii inside. Tan Arizona out here, but for the touch of green of a paloverde tree sprouting from where the motor of a sixty-something Ford should have been. The car had to have been parked there for at least a decade. Heather reached up and knocked on the door.

"That you, Angel?"

Heather made a noncommittal noise and the door swung in. A man opened the screen and stood there in a bathrobe. Polyester, covered with a bold paisley pattern designed to induce nausea. The man was short and skinny, except for a protruding belly. Pale, scrawny legs and knobby knees beneath his robe. Dirty toenails completed the romantic effect, in a pair of mismatched flip flops. And he held a tray on which stood a pitcher and saguaro-armed margarita glasses.

"Where…?"

Heather grabbed the hem of his robe and tugged. Not hard, but the thing was already arranged to be open enough to display his hollow chest. And its belt must have been loose, for Angel's convenience. It pulled open and displayed something even scrawnier than his legs.

"What…Who…?" And then he spun and tried to dart back into the trailer. The margaritas rained onto the concrete blocks and the pitcher and glasses tumbled into the dust. He didn't get far. Heather still held the hem of his robe and it pulled away from him—revealing a skinny butt adorned with pimples—before he reached the end of the cloth. His feet came out from under him and he fell hard. Heather followed him inside. Belatedly, he tried to cover himself. For which Heather was grateful. He had small hands, but no problem hiding his miniscule manhood.

"You can't come in here," he squeaked. "I know my rights."

"Flashing is against the law," she told him. "I witnessed a crime in progress. That gives me the right."

"But…" he stammered, "but nobody was supposed to see me except Angel. Where is she?"

Heather shook her head. Elvis was something else. Something from the rodent family, maybe, except that was an insult to rats.

"I've got no idea where Angel is," Heather told him, kicking his robe so that it covered a little more of his repulsive nudity. "If she's lucky, she's having a root canal instead of a date with you."

He gathered the thin fabric closer.

"You tore my robe off. If I was exposed, it's your fault, not mine. Now what do you want?"

Heather took another step inside. Close enough to loom over him, especially since she was taller and a lot more muscular. Close enough so one of her boots was on the hem of that robe, making it certain he couldn't go anywhere. She put her hand on the butt of her service weapon and let her eyes take in the trailer's interior. A dusty iridescent nude painted on black velvet and a spread—unfortunately, precisely the right word—centerfold of Miss October, 2006, decorated his walls. That was the classy stuff. His furniture deserved to be out in the yard with the other junk. The place appeared empty except for him. And he cowered in a way that made it seem unlikely he thought anyone would come to his rescue.

"Let's start with that ring you ordered from Colors."

His expression changed. Before she could decide what that meant he kicked her in the knee and grabbed for something behind the door. Something, Heather thought as she stumbled, that looked very much like a MAC 10 .45-caliber machine pistol.

◇◇◇

When Mad Dog's mind and body reconnected, he was in the rear of some kind of vehicle. A van, he thought. He was on a metal floor, and it hurt whenever they went over bumps. He lay on his back with his arms behind him. He tried to move them and discovered they were secured that way. His legs were bound, too.

"Why are you doing this?" Mad Dog called to the driver. It didn't exactly come out clearly. Mad Dog's mouth and vocal cords weren't as fully in touch with his brain as they should be. Still, the kid who'd tasered him answered.

"I'm the only one who can hear you, so stuff a sock in it. If you don't, I'll come back and literally stuff a sock in it."

Mad Dog decided to be quiet. The kid had proved to be a man of his word so far. If Mad Dog pushed his head back, he could see the top of the windshield at the front of the truck. And out of it, not one damn thing that was useful. Just clouds. He couldn't even tell where the sun was to get an idea of what direction they were going.

The van came to a sudden stop. Mad Dog slid forward and bumped his head on something. The truck started again, turned, and palm fronds swept across his view. No help there. Palms like that were all over Tucson. But there was something about the sound of the truck that seemed familiar. He'd heard it before. In fact, he'd heard it that morning when the horn sounded and he got out of his sweat lodge to see who was there and it had been a brown truck, almost lost to view. UPS, he'd thought then. And UPS, he thought now. He was in a UPS truck, or something like it.

They bounced and twisted and turned for what seemed like an eternity. And then they stopped again. A door slid open near the truck—a big one—and they pulled inside some kind of building. The motor went silent. The big door slid closed again and all Mad Dog could see through the top of the windshield was a corrugated-metal roof, far above. The driver blocked the light as he stepped over Mad Dog and opened the rear door.

"Where you want him?"

"In there," a second voice responded. "Take his head, I'll get his feet."

"Where am I?" Mad Dog said. "What's going on?"

The man who took his feet had a buzz cut, a short gray mustache, and pale gray eyes.

"Heavy son'a'bitch, ain't he?"

Mad Dog got a glimpse of a UPS logo on the side of the truck before they took him through another door into a small, dark room. They put him on a row of sacks that shifted a little under him as if they were filled with seeds or grain. Then the two men turned, retracing their steps. They shut the door behind them, leaving him in total darkness.

"Hey," Mad Dog shouted. "At least cut me loose."

They didn't answer, but he heard a shushing sound from somewhere across the room.

"Please don't shout, mister," a tiny voice said. It sounded young, like it belonged to a child, maybe. "You don't want them coming back in here. If they come, it'll be with a cattle prod. I learned that the hard way."

◇◇◇

Mrs. Kraus stood at the top of a dizzying staircase. Monstrous spiders scuttled up and down the steps, waiting to pounce as soon as she descended. And her armor had taken too many hits. It was all but worn out. She wasn't sure her avatar, Femfatale, could make it. The way this quest was going, Fem might have to resurrect at a graveyard and suffer the penalty that made her an easy kill for fifteen minutes. Bummer!

"'Scuse me, Ms. Kraus," a voice said behind her.

The shock of finding someone in the office on a day she'd assumed the courthouse was empty caused her to jump almost high enough to leave fingernail scratches when she tried to grab the ceiling. And to make her wish she'd done more about those cholesterol and blood pressure problems Doc Jones warned her about at her last physical. It didn't exactly calm her to discover there were two of them and both carried assault weapons. The guns weren't pointed at her, though, and that made her wonder if she could get her Glock out of her purse and take the pair out before they cut her in half.

"Could you tell us, please, is the sheriff here?"

Why, it was only Ned Evans and his brother Zeke. Farmers she'd known most of her life. But what the hell were they doing here on Christmas Day with weapons like that? And dressed in funny uniforms all covered with camouflage.

"Englishman's not home, neither," Ned said. His voice was even softer and gentler than his brother's. "Do you happen to know where he might be?"

It took Mrs. Kraus a minute to be sure her heart hadn't exploded. "He's on an investigation," she said, catching a little attitude along with her breath. She didn't much like to share departmental business with the general public, no matter how well armed.

"Is he working alone, or does he have assistance on this particular investigation?" Ned asked.

"Assistance? Are you kidding? On our budget? You two have got quite a sense of humor."

Actually, they didn't, and while their voices had been soft enough, there was a kind of hardness to their expressions she didn't care for. She didn't care for the other two men, either. They were equally armed and uniformed as they crossed her line of vision just out in the foyer beyond the open sheriff's office door.

"We heard," Ned said, "he might have help from an outside agency. You know who that might be?"

"And how many agents are with him?" Zeke added.

"I don't know what you boys are talking about," Mrs. Kraus said. "Englishman's out there on his own, just like usual. Now, what are you and those other people doing here and why are you carrying guns like these?"

Something caught the corner of her vision. Something bright and yellow moved in the wind, just outside the window. A flag. Someone was raising a flag on the pole in front of the courthouse. It had a snake on it. And words. DON'T TREAD ON ME!

"We're insuring the security of a free state, ma'am," Zeke said.

Ned nodded. "I'm afraid, for the moment, we've got to assume you're part of the threat to our freedom. You'll have to hand over that Glock you carry."

Mrs. Kraus couldn't believe it. She reached down, slow and easy, picked up her purse and opened it. She drew the Glock, even slower and easier. She didn't hand it over though. She was seething inside. She pointed the 9mm toward the Evans brothers. "You want my gun?" she said. "You know exactly how you're going to have to take it."

"You mean?" Ned asked.

Mrs. Kraus straightened her spine. She stood proud and tall, as dangerous as Femfatale, even at less than five feet. "That's right. Pried from my cold dead fingers."

◇◇◇

Heather had already lost her balance when the MAC 10 came out. She was falling away from Elvis, not toward him. Going for the gun was out of the question. So was counting on the notorious shortcomings of the MAC. It was a cheap, inaccurate weapon that threw a horrendous amount of lead at its target in a very short time—one of the reasons gangsters and terrorists loved it.

Heather had one option. The door. She dived for it.

The MAC went off like Krakatoa. Lead whistled through the open door and hacksawed a pair of swaths through the metal on either side. As Heather hit the ground, she pushed back under the trailer. Not that it was safe there. The floor was cheap plywood that wouldn't stop a hail of bullets any better than the walls of the trailer had. The floor sagged as Elvis scrambled to his feet and hustled his pimpled backside against the wall beside the door.

Her SIG Sauer was in her hand, pointed up. Up, almost exactly, at the sagging plywood. She should order him to drop his weapon first, but if she gave away her location, the MAC might rip a massive hole in the floor, and not do her any good either.

The SIG's magazine held fifteen rounds. Heather put eight into a circle about eighteen inches across. The MAC didn't answer. In fact, she heard it fall to the dirty linoleum floor. She heard Elvis fall, too, probably not in the best of shape.

To be safe, she rolled to her right and came out from under the trailer several feet to the side of the door. Gun up and ready, she edged along the trailer's side until she saw Elvis. Or what had been Elvis. His face was turned toward her. Only one eye remained and it was already cloudy. She focused the SIG on that eye and went back inside.

Elvis was a mess. It looked like every bullet had hit him somewhere. There were holes in his feet, a shattered knee, an arm nearly torn loose from the shoulder. And that little something he'd hoped to share with Angel wasn't there anymore.

Heather resisted an urge to add her breakfast to the gore now covering much of the interior. Instead, she kicked the MAC over into a corner, and searched the rest of the trailer to be sure it contained no other threats. Then she went back to the door to see if their little war had raised anyone's curiosity.

The wind whispered through the paloverde that sprouted out of the Ford. There were no other signs of life. No sirens in the distance. She let herself begin to relax a little. Not enough, since she swung around and nearly squeezed off more rounds into Elvis when her cell phone vibrated.

◇◇◇

The professional jaywalked across Stone as soon as Bill and his pickup were gone. He retrieved a magnetic key holder from under the fender of a Dodge Ram three-quarter ton pickup truck parked beside a statue of Paul Bunyan in an otherwise empty parking lot. Not exactly who he'd expected to meet in southern Arizona.

The keys to the truck and to a Ninja 650R motorcycle strapped into the bed behind the cab, were inside. He drove the Dodge across the street. Parked it with the passenger's side door near the back entrance to the former TV repair store, and went in.

He brought in a small package from the Dodge. From it, he took a large, very strong magnet. When he got close to Mouse's computer, the magnet jumped from his hands and dented the processor's case. The computer's screen went blank as the magnet rearranged every byte on the hard drive. It was unlikely anyone would be able to view what the security cameras had recorded after this. Not that the professional cared. It would just fit the investigating officers' expectations and stimulate their imaginations. If he came to southern Arizona again, he would look completely different—unrecognizable. He didn't wipe any surface he'd touched. His fingerprints had been surgically removed years ago.

He dragged Mouse's goons out and into the Ram's cab, strapping them in with seatbelts so they stayed upright. He stuck a pair of cheap billed caps low on their heads so what little traffic he encountered wouldn't notice the slack looks on their faces.

Before Mouse and Cowboy moved against him, *Rabioso* had gone to earth in a safe house in the Catalina Vista neighborhood of central Tucson. It was an upscale neighborhood. Some of the houses were surrounded by walls. *Rabioso*'s was walled and gated with solid slabs of artfully rusted iron thick enough to stop nearly any bullet. *Rabioso* felt safe hiding behind it. He shouldn't have.

Rabioso was one of the professional's clients. Just like Mouse had been. Just as Cowboy might still assume himself to be. But *Rabioso* had already paid a million up front. And expected to pay another. He, after all, was the one whose empire was being threatened by two others.

In fact, the professional's clients numbered in the dozens. When the governor-elect served as a sheriff he'd made many enemies. Enough for the professional to pick up several contracts on the man's life. Five and six figure deals resulting in lots of satisfied customers who would never know how many others had paid for the same result.

Though most of the professional's clients in this little drug war would be double-crossed and the professional would not receive their final payments, this would be a very profitable day. And the real beauty of it was that he was being paid by scores of people to do things that allowed him to accomplish his own goal. It was the perfect storm, and he was managing it to a perfect climax. He'd left the girl a note so she had to realize he was coming for her. Did she realize how soon? He could hardly contain his impatience. One last detail....

The professional had called ahead. When he pulled up in front of the iron gate, two of *Rabioso*'s men opened it. They helped him take the motorcycle out of the bed and park it at the curb outside. Then they closed the gate and, hidden by high walls, helped him lug Mouse's men into the living room.

Rabioso waited for him there, standing beside a cheerfully blazing fire. The drug lord was a big man who resembled Mad Dog a little, except for his mane of silver hair. They were the same size and build. And, despite his nickname, *Rabioso* was another Anglo. The border drug trade was an equal opportunity employer.

"Mouse is dead," the professional said. "I brought you two of his goons. They saw me kill him so they may be willing to change sides. Give you information to help you pull down whatever's left of Mouse's organization."

"Amazing," *Rabioso* said. "I didn't think you could pull this off."

"Or we can leave their bodies here. Part of the next phase. Do you have the unmatched pair of silenced automatic weapons I requested?"

Rabioso sent one of his men to get them.

"And product? Is there some in the house?"

"Yes. In the garage. It makes me nervous, having it here, but your idea of making Cowboy think I've been killed in a shootout with Mouse's forces will give me the element of surprise I need to move against him."

"And help you afford my fee," the professional said. He examined the weapons. Cheap throw-aways that offended him. He preferred to work with tools of the finest quality.

"You should leave so I can get on with this," the professional said, checking over each of the weapons, seeing that the silencers were properly affixed so they wouldn't explode when he began using them. Checking their actions. Seeing that the magazines were full.

"Shall we move your truck or do you want to leave it here?"

"Here." The professional was satisfied. Both guns would work well enough to do what he needed.

"But it's blocking my car," *Rabioso* explained.

"Oh," the professional turned and looked out the picture window with its one-way glass. The truck was where he wanted it. So were *Rabioso* and his men. All together in the living room.

"It's not a problem," the professional said, and opened up with one of the guns. *Rabioso* and his men went down like stones, and just as dead. The professional turned the other weapon on Mouse's sleeping muscle, further decorating the room in holiday crimson. Here was another final payment, a million dollars that would not come his way. Oh well. He had never planned to collect it.

He moved the bodies around a little. Artfully placed a few more bullets. Back outside, he tattooed the house with bullet holes. Then turned the other gun on the truck. The weapon chattered but the sound of bullets striking metal was far louder.

When he was through, he placed one gun with Palmer. The other he gave to *Rabioso*. Making certain, in both cases, their fingerprints were on the weapons. He caused each to fire one last round for the paraffin tests. Then he double-checked the garage. Product was, indeed, stored there. Finally, he set his explosives. Four incendiaries in the house. One much larger device, in the Dodge. And some surprises for the bomb squad. Duds, but complex enough to keep them busy and complicate the investigation.

When the professional was done, he opened the gate and mounted the Ninja. The neighborhood remained quiet. Apparently no one had noticed the silenced shots or recognized the ring of bullets into the Dodge.

The motorcycle took him away, its whine far louder than the noise of the fatal drama he left behind. He was half-a-mile down the road when the bombs began going off. The neighborhood would notice now.

◇◇◇

"Hey, Heather. It's Brad."

As if she wouldn't recognize his voice.

"I'm sorry to bother you on what has to be a crazy day for you, but Captain Matus called me. He's looking for you."

That surprised her.

"Why didn't he just call me?"

"I had the impression he got a little frustrated at not being able to get a signal on his phone. Threw it at a boulder. Now it doesn't work at all. He wants you to call him right away. I'll give you his new number. You got something to write on?"

She looked down at the blood pooling around Elvis. She could write in his blood, she supposed. She gave herself a mental slap for succumbing to that little burst of hysteria.

"No," Heather said.

"Oh. Well, you can call me back when you do. Or call your headquarters."

Heather's mind was beginning to function again. "Why didn't he just call headquarters? Get my number from them?"

"They're a little short-handed. You do know Governor Hyde was murdered, don't you?"

"Yes." Heather knew.

"Captain Matus says the person handling the office can't find the phone list or your employment file, or even his butt with both hands in broad daylight."

She'd heard Matus use that expression before.

"Anyway, he said it's important and you need to call him right away. I hope this won't interfere with tonight?"

"Tonight?"

"You know. Dinner. Late snack, actually. Leftovers. My folks are expecting you, and you don't want to back out on an appointment with the senator at the last minute. Dad is not the forgiving sort. And Niki flew in from college today. I really want you to meet Niki. And she wants to meet...."

She interrupted him. "I've got a lot going on."

"It's important to me, so just try, please."

She had no time for argument or explanation. "Sure," she said. "I'll do my best. Give me Matus' number and I'll start trying to clear things away."

Brad did. She hung up and dialed it before she could forget.

"Matus," her boss answered.

"English," she replied.

"Where are you? We need that letter and the envelope you found with the governor's skin. We've set up a mobile command post just off 286 on the edge of the reservation. Right by the turnoff to where you found Hyde. How soon can you get here?"

Heather looked at Elvis. "Probably not real quick. I've got a problem I have to deal with."

"I'm sorry," the Captain said. "That's right. What was the deal with Mad Dog? Couldn't you straighten that out?"

"No," she said, and gave him the Cliffs Notes version of her day so far, including Elvis.

He made a reference to the Prince of Peace, though she didn't think it was birthday greeting or prayer. "Okay. You in the city or the county?"

She wasn't sure. The borders got complicated down here. She gave him the address.

"Hang on a minute. Let me figure out who's got jurisdiction and see how we can expedite this."

Heather held. It was December, but a couple of flies had already found Elvis. Maybe all God's creatures deserved a Christmas feast.

She looked out the door. Still no indication anyone had seen or heard the exchange of gunfire, or thought it unusual if they had. No sirens. And then the Captain was back.

"Damn, girl. Our county sheriff wants your hide." Matus paused a moment. "That was a poor choice of words under these circumstances. Sheriff thinks you're purposefully trying to mess up his investigation. Not our investigation, you'll note. The sheriff has it in his head you refused to cooperate with a deputy, then disturbed a crime scene to turn in human remains in a fashion that may inhibit prosecution. His words. He wants to know where you are so he can send units to bring you in. So, I didn't tell him. Has any law enforcement responded to your situation so far? Did you call this shooting in yet?"

"No, sir. It happened right before Brad called to give me this number. You're the first to know."

"Keep it that way. String crime tape at the entrances. Close the gate. Tape it, too. Then drive straight down here and bring me that letter. If you're on the reservation, I can control the situation, make sure they question you as a duly constituted law enforcement officer operating under orders. I'll start paving the way. Maybe the sheriff won't be so angry by the time you get here. Lord knows, he's got plenty of other things to be upset about."

"What about Uncle Mad Dog?"

This time Matus was the one who paused. "You got more leads?"

Maybe if she searched this place. But that could take hours. "Not right now," she admitted.

"Then get that letter down here. I'll find a way to help with Mad Dog. Re-establish a little interdepartmental cooperation, maybe."

Heather had a bad feeling. If she went in, she wouldn't be allowed to look for her uncle once the sheriff's department got its hands on her. But she didn't know what else to do. Captain Matus seemed to read her mind.

"No buts. I'll smuggle you out of here in an unmarked vehicle if it comes to that. Mad Dog is my friend and I won't let him down. So, get yourself here right now."

"Yes, sir," she agreed. Her mind reserved the right to think more about those buts, though.

◇◇◇

Mrs. Kraus wasn't sure she could make herself kill either of them. But she was a good shot. She decided she'd shoot to wound if they tried to take her gun, then hunker down behind her desk because a great many bullets would likely fly into the sheriff's office from all those guns out in the foyer.

"I can't do it, Ned," Zeke Evans said. "I mean, we're trying to do to her just what we're trying to prevent."

"Yeah, Zeke, but she's government. She's one of Englishman's people and he's the one who started confiscating guns."

"She's not a deputy," Zeke said.

Mrs. Kraus wasn't surprised to see the pair arguing with each other. The brothers usually did that. But they usually argued about financial matters, the two being partners in a farming venture that had been one bad harvest away from bankruptcy for nearly as long as she could remember. This time, she was their subject, and they were treating her as if she weren't there. Even though she stood right in front of them, 9 mm Glock in hand.

"She's just Englishman's secretary."

"Office manager," Mrs. Kraus corrected Ned and harrumphed at the insult. "And what's that crap you said about seizing guns? Englishman isn't seizing guns."

Ned continued to ignore her. "Anybody works for Englishman has to be part of the plan. How we gonna stop it if we leave the enemies of freedom armed?"

"Well, you take her gun, then," Zeke said. "I'm not gonna do it. She's got just as much right to carry hers as we do to carry ours."

"She's not a militia," Ned countered.

"And we're not much of one ourselves. Not that we have to be. That's not what the Second Amendment says. It says we get to keep our guns in case we need to form a milita. Mrs. Kraus has as much right to do that as you and me. You still wanna confiscate her gun?"

"Nah, I guess not," Ned said. "You go ahead and watch your TV cartoons, Mrs. Kraus. We'll just kind of take control of the courthouse until our free state is secure again. But that means you can't use them phones."

TV? Cartoons? That gave Mrs. Kraus an idea. But she still felt compelled to rip them new assholes first.

"Ned Evans," she said. "You are a damn fool. What if your house gets broke into while you're here playing soldier? What if your wife's life is at risk? Who's she gonna call? Sheriff's office, that's who. And if I don't answer, how we gonna get help to her?"

"That's not likely to happen," Ned said.

"Probably not," Mrs. Kraus said. "But I would have sworn this morning that our courthouse would not be invaded by a bunch of nitwits with their own flag on this Christmas Day. And yet here you are."

"She's got you there, Ned." Zeke said. "So why don't you stay here and keep an eye on her? Make sure she don't warn the sheriff, and you take any calls she gets. How's that?"

"What're you gonna do, Zeke?"

"Me, I think I'll find Commandant Koestel and see if he don't think we should set up some kind of mess hall so's we don't miss our Christmas dinners."

Ned seemed to think that was a fine idea and Zeke left the office. Mrs. Kraus sat in front of the computer, pistol in her lap. Her adrenaline rush was fading and her knees had turned a little wobbly.

On her screen, Femfatale hadn't moved and the spiders on the staircase hadn't found her yet. Not that Mrs. Kraus much cared about the game just now, not in the usual sense. But that thing they'd said about cartoons.... Maybe Fem, a level seventy-four Night Elf witch, could cast a spell that reached right out of the game to save Englishman. She looked at Ned sitting there with his goofy smile and assault rifle. Why not?

◇◇◇

"Who are you?" Mad Dog whispered to the little voice in the dark. "Why are you here? What's going on? Who are these people?"

He made himself shut up. That was too much to ask. He needed to reassure his fellow prisoner, not make things worse with his own panic.

"My name is Cassie," she said. "Daddy and I got kidnapped. I don't know who did it or why, and I don't know why you're here. Do you work for the state?"

The part about the state puzzled him. "No," he said. "Why?"

She was silent for a moment. Wondering, he decided, whether she could trust him. At least that's what her response indicated.

"Tell me who *you* are, first. Why you think you might be here."

"My name is Mad Dog," he said. Then realized how that might sound under the circumstances. Like he was some gangster himself. Or a member of a rival gang. "It's my real name," he explained, and went on to tell her how he changed it after picking up the nickname as a football player in high school. How his father had run off and his mother was Cheyenne and he wanted to be Cheyenne, too. How he'd tried, not just to find his place in the tribal culture, but to develop his skills as a shaman.

"What's a shaman?" she asked.

"Kind of a magician," he said. "A wizard. As to why I'm here…I don't know. I think somebody confused me with someone else. A package got delivered to my house this morning." He decided not to explain what was in it. "It wasn't for me, but a sheriff's deputy showed up and then a lawyer, and things got really confusing. I ended up going with the lawyer. She thought I was some criminal, so I left her place and got caught by a guy in a uniform with what I thought was a toy gun. He stunned me with it and brought me here."

"You don't have anything to do with Arizona government?"

"No. I'm from Kansas. Been living here awhile, but haven't changed my residence."

"Oh, I thought state government might be the link." Her voice whispered right in his ear now. She'd crossed the room. She must not be bound. "Would you like me to help you get those plastic handcuffs off?"

"Sure, but you have to have scissors or a sharp knife, don't you?"

"Not when you've got a safety pin."

He felt her hand touch his face, his shoulder, then slide down his arm. "You'll have to roll on your side so I can get at your hands."

Mad Dog rolled.

"See," Cassie said, "these draw tie things use a really strong roller lock. But if you've got something small enough, like my safety pin, you can push it in and release the lock. Pull the plastic cables back through, like this."

Mad Dog felt the plastic relax against his right wrist. He pulled his hand free.

"Don't move too much. I've got to get the other side. Then your feet."

"How did you know that?" Mad Dog asked.

"Daddy has bodyguards. Most of them are snooty. They don't like kids. But this one guy is different. He showed me. You'd be surprised how many things you can do with a safety pin. So I always wear one."

Mad Dog pulled his left hand free and she moved to his feet.

"Bodyguards? Why does your dad have bodyguards?"

"He's the new Governor of Arizona," she said. "I bet he's sorry we didn't bring along some of those guys."

With his feet free, Mad Dog sat up on a sack, found the edge of the stack, and dropped his shoes to the floor. "Thanks," he said. He thought about getting up, but he didn't know where he should go. He couldn't see a thing in here.

"I've already explored the room," she said as she sat beside him. "There's no way out but that door they brought you in."

"Your dad's the governor? Really?"

"Yeah."

"Well, what were you two doing on Christmas Day when you got kidnapped? And why didn't you have a bodyguard?"

"It was yesterday, actually. Daddy said he'd take me hiking. Just me and him, one last time before he takes office. It's a zoo when he goes places now. So he slipped his security and the reporters in Phoenix and drove down here. I told Mom some friends were taking me to a movie and met him, instead. Only then he got a phone call. He said it was a guy he had to see but it wouldn't take a minute. We pulled in behind a strip mall, and all of a sudden there were a bunch of men in uniforms with guns and…."

She snuffled a little and Mad Dog put his arm around her.

"They took Daddy somewhere else when they stuck me in here. They left me by myself ever since. Until they brought you. You didn't see my daddy out there when they brought you in, did you?"

"No. I'm sorry. But are you saying they didn't even feed you? They haven't brought you water?"

"They left a few water bottles and some candy bars beside me. And my hands were cuffed in front, which made it a lot easier to get free. When I heard them at the door just now, I slipped the cuffs back on. Say, are you hungry or thirsty? I've still got some water and candy."

"No, thanks," Mad Dog said.

"I wonder if they'll come again. Or if they're just going to leave us here to die. I'm afraid for Daddy. I wish you could use some of your magic and get us out of here."

Mad Dog hugged her. "Well, I can try."

Most of Mad Dog's magic was related to his wolf-hybrid, Hailey. He was convinced she was a *Nissimon*—a Cheyenne spirit animal much like a witch's familiar. He closed his eyes—not that he needed to in this total darkness—and thought about her. Concentrated on her. His mind found a spark of brilliant light and took him to it. He recognized it. Hailey. He told her he was in trouble. She already knew.

"Do you hear that?" Cassie said.

Mad Dog opened his eyes and realized he did hear something. It sounded like someone was digging against the side of the building. Someone or something. Like a dog, maybe.

Or a wolf.

◇◇◇

Sergeant Parker walked into Tucson Police Headquarters and put Mad Dog's cell phone on her desk. The place was in total chaos. Her captain ran up, demanded, "Where have you been?"

He wasn't angry, just agitated. Still, she felt compelled to justify her absence, even if she wasn't on duty.

"Looking into a possible kidnapping," she said. Mad Dog was an odd enough character that she'd planned to put in calls to his girlfriend and maybe his brother before making the matter official. The captain put all that on hold.

"I need you and Anderson to join your unit right now. They're ready to roll. A series of bombs just leveled a residence up near the Arizona Inn. First responders report bags of what looks like cocaine all over the neighborhood. And the bullet-riddled body of a known soldier for one of the drug bosses. The fire has several sources. Probably incendiary devices. We need you and your people up there in case there are more."

"Yes, sir," Parker snapped. "On our way."

The Captain put a hand on her arm before she could follow Anderson out the door to the bomb truck.

"Parker," he said. "We don't know what's going on, but this could be big. The body—it's one of *Rabioso*'s men. And we've got units at a storefront on North Stone where an anonymous caller told us we'd find one of *Rabioso's* chief rivals. Mouse is dead. You know what that means, Sergeant?"

On a day that started when the flayed skin of Arizona's governor elect had been discovered, it could mean almost anything.

"Right this minute," the captain said, "what we've feared could actually be happening. Mexico's drug wars may be spilling over the border. And Tucson, God help us, might be ground zero."

◇◇◇

Sheriff English examined the Porter's lighted flag decoration—rope lights in patriotic red and white and blue, with several of the ropes shattered. He checked the smooth pebbles that had apparently caused the breaks. Dave still wouldn't allow the sheriff onto his property, but Marian had given the sheriff a steaming mug of coffee and an apologetic smile when she brought out Dave's bag full of evidence.

"Why do you say slingshot?" the sheriff asked. "Somebody could have sneaked up close to the house before you walled your yard off. Thrown these rocks."

"I heard the stones hit," Dave said. "Ran out the front door in time to see a car take off. Had to have been shot from clear out here. That's way too far for an accurate throw."

"You didn't tell me you saw the car. Did you get a license number? Could you tell what make it was?"

"No. Dark night and their lights were off. American V8, though. From the sound of it. Big block Chevy, maybe."

The sheriff had more questions but his cell rang.

"I'm sorry," English said. "I'm always on duty."

"Go right ahead, sheriff," Marian said. Dave nodded and the sheriff took the call.

"Englishman?" an unfamiliar voice asked.

The sheriff didn't much like the nickname. "Sheriff English," he said.

"'Kay," the voice said. "That's cool." He read off the sheriff's number, area code included. "Is that who I'm talking to?"

The sheriff acknowledged that it was.

"Then I've got a message from Fem."

The sheriff didn't know a Fem. "Who?"

"Femfatale, she's a Night Elf witch. Said it was real important."

"Yes?" the sheriff said, though he may have sounded doubtful.

"Tell Englishman the courthouse has been taken by gun nuts. Tell him Kraus is a prisoner, but still armed. At least half-a-dozen men with automatic weapons, but Kraus will support from the rear.

"Sounds way cool. I'd like to hear more about this after I level my death knight. Taking a courthouse full of terrorists, man, that's gotta be some kind of fun."

"Uh, right," the sheriff said.

"Whoa, just got an invitation to a random dungeon," the voice said. "Gotta go. Good luck, man."

"Wait, this Fem…?" the sheriff began, but the line had gone dead.

"Something wrong, Sheriff?" Dave Porter asked.

"Yeah. Somebody says the courthouse has been seized by a bunch of people with automatic weapons and they're holding Mrs. Kraus hostage."

"Dave isn't part of that crazy militia," Marian said. "We decided to just defend our own place. Dave's not going out looking for trouble like them others."

"You know about this?" the sheriff said, incredulous. "You mean it's real?"

Neither of the Porters would meet his eyes. Dave scuffed his feet in the snow again.

The sheriff had his answer. It was not one he liked.

◇◇◇

When the claws stopped scratching dirt and metal, Mad Dog and Cassie were no longer in the dark. A small hole had appeared at the base of a wall. Mad Dog bent and examined it. The wall of the building overlapped its concrete floor by about an inch. The metal wall also extended a few inches below the concrete and beneath the ground's surface. Or it had, before Hailey started digging.

"More, Hailey," Mad Dog whispered into the hole. But no more digging occurred. In fact, there was no evidence his wolf was still out there. Though he felt sure he'd been in contact with her, somehow, he was no longer certain Hailey had done the digging. Some other dog, perhaps. Members of *Canis lupus* had seemed to do Hailey favors from time to time—even at the cost of their lives. "Who" actually dug the hole didn't matter. He knew Hailey caused it. And now, they could see a little.

"Wow," Cassie breathed in his ear. "That was cool. Will your magic make that dog dig us an escape route?"

"I don't think so. It may have gotten us started, but I think we have to take it from here."

Cassie didn't seem disappointed. He got a look at her for the first time—cute kid, confident, with hope sparkling in her eyes.

"You're bald," she said. He realized she must be getting a good look at him for the first time, too.

"And you're brunette, which is what I used to be before I started shaving my head like Yul Brynner."

"Who?"

Fame, Mad Dog realized, was a generational thing.

"Never mind." He stood and let his eyes adjust to the less-than-total darkness. The sacks they'd laid him on were horse feed. Fifty-pound bags, he thought. Several brands and varieties. Either someone raised horses here or whoever owned the place was in the business of supplying horse owners. Cassie had been on a stack of hay bales. The old fashioned rectangular bales, not the huge circular ones that had become the norm back in Kansas. But neither of those sights interested him as much as what he noticed hanging along the opposite wall—tools. A shovel, wide mouthed, the kind you'd scoop manure with. A broom. A pitchfork. And, as he got closer, a pair of hay hooks—short curved spikes of metal with handles so you could hook a hay bale and lift or drag it. Not ideal for what Mad Dog had in mind, but possibly adequate.

He gathered the collection and carried them back to the hole that had become their light source.

"What are you going to do?" Cassie asked.

"Make the hole larger," Mad Dog said. "Our size, maybe."

He bent and examined the base of the outside wall again. Corrugated steel. It would be hard to bend it with the tools he had. And he couldn't pound on it. That would bring the bad guys with their cattle prod.

But it looked like there was a seam beside the hole. A spot where two pieces of corrugated metal overlapped.

"If I only had a little more light."

"Does this help?"

Mad Dog's eyes blinked in the sudden blinding glare. He looked up. Fluorescents lined the ceiling. And Cassie stood with her hand on the light switch beside the door. The one he should have realized had to be there. Duh!

"Yeah," he said. "Thanks."

There was a seam, all right. He tried one of the hay hooks and managed to work it between the pieces of metal. He strained, pushed. The hook scraped against steel, but the steel yielded.

"Well, what do you know," Mad Dog said. "This might actually work."

◇◇◇

Mrs. Kraus beat Ned Evans to the phone when it rang. Then danced around her desk to keep him from grabbing it.

"Benteen County Sheriff's Office."

Ned whispered, "Careful what you say." He came around the desk and got his ear near enough to hear the voice on the other side of the connection.

"Mrs. Kraus. This is Sergeant Parker in Tucson."

Mrs. Kraus heard the wail of a siren in the background.

"I'm in the middle of an emergency," Parker said, "but I thought Englishman should know…." That was all Mrs. Kraus caught before Ned changed his mind and took the phone.

"Yes, Ma'am," Ned said. "We'll tell him."

"What is it? What's going on?" Mrs. Kraus tried to take the phone back but Ned was too strong for her.

"We got a couple of minor problems here," Ned said. "Mrs. Kraus is on the other line. Who, me? Why I'm the new deputy. Ned…uh, Ned Smith."

"Ned Evans, give me that phone. Let me speak to Pauline Parker this instant." Mrs. Kraus raised her voice hoping Parker could hear her. Ned glared and one of the militia men in the foyer looked in to see what was going on.

"No. No problem. I'll tell the sheriff," Ned said. Then he said ouch when Mrs. Kraus kicked him in the shin and yanked the phone out of his fingers.

"Pauline? Pauline? You still there?"

Parker was gone, though. And Mrs. Kraus had no idea whether Parker had understood Mrs. Kraus intentionally called her by the wrong first name. Pauline—it was the best Mrs. Kraus could manage on the spur of the moment. The Perils of Pauline were silent movie serials, dating back to even before Mrs. Kraus' time. Sergeant Parker might not know about them. Might just think the years had taken their toll and the old woman back in Benteen County had forgotten her real name.

Or Parker could be too busy with her own emergency, so the wrong name wouldn't even register. But it might, and if Parker realized Mrs. Kraus intentionally missed her name she'd understand Mrs. Kraus needed help. Just like the heroine in those ancient motion pictures, whether Parker caught the reference or not.

Ned took the phone out of Mrs. Kraus' hand and put it back in its cradle. "Don't answer it again," he said.

Harvey Koestel strode into the sheriff's office. "Who called?" he asked. He carried some kind of automatic rifle that looked like it held about a million rounds. His uniform had stars on the shoulders and was topped with a gray Civil War kepi, a Confederate battle flag pinned above the visor.

"Someone from Tucson. About Mad Dog." Ned stepped over to the counter and filled Koestel in on the details, conveniently standing with his back to Mrs. Kraus and whispering so she couldn't hear. Very slowly, she lifted the receiver back off its hook. The dial tone sounded incredibly loud to her. Not loud enough to alert the cream of this Kansas country-boy militia, though. She was going to dial Englishman, but she suddenly saw a bright fuchsia message in the War of Worldcraft's usual shorthand appear on her computer screen where Femfatale now faced a swarm of lavender hornets, each the size of a St. Bernard.

"called eman. gave message. tell me bout game u 2 r in soon. got 2 go 2 dungeon. brb."

So Englishman had been warned. But he'd need help. Who would understand and believe there was serious trouble here with the fewest words? Who would care enough to be sure to do something about it? Easy, she decided. Heather, in far off Arizona. Her fingers danced across the phone's key pad.

Ned slammed his palm down, killing the call before she got a connection. Koestel stuck the muzzle of his machine gun in her throat.

"Who'd you call?"

Mrs. Kraus turned and glared into his eyes with an intensity that should have turned his heart to ice.

"Do your mothers know how much trouble you boys are in?"

◇◇◇

Just-the-family Christmas dinner at the Cole's turned into a disaster. The senator took call after call. By the time Niki finally persuaded him to sit at the table, the mashed potatoes were cold, the salad had wilted, the turkey was overcooked, and Mrs. Cole wobbled from sampling the cooking sherry. It didn't help much when the phone rang again midway through the senator's efforts to carve his way to a piece of meat moister than cardboard.

"Don't answer it," Mrs. Cole said. As usual, the senator ignored her. He'd brought a phone to the table, evidently anticipating more news.

Brad sighed. Niki rolled her eyes. Brad thought she'd been away from home too long if she expected an idealized version of their normal family meals.

"Senator Cole," their father barked into the receiver. Mrs. Cole lifted her wine glass, saluted everyone at the table, and drained it.

"Yes," the senator said. He said it several more times while his wife refilled and re-emptied her glass. Heather would get an instructional introduction to the Cole family if the day continued like this.

The senator finally put the phone down. "I don't believe it. All hell seems to be breaking loose today. That was the mayor." Tucson's mayor, Brad assumed. Greater Tucson had Balkanized a few decades ago. It consisted of half-a-dozen interconnected and competing communities now. Tucson was by far the largest, though. The senator wasn't apt to take a mid-Christmas dinner call from the mayor of Marana.

The Coles, however, didn't live in any of the metropolitan areas. Their home lay in the foothills, an unincorporated suburb on the north side of Tucson where the wealthy had fled as municipal neighborhoods began containing diverse populations that reflected the rest of Southern Arizona. They really were foothills—the lower reaches of the Santa Catalina range. The area wasn't as exclusive as it had once been, but there were still gated communities, like this one, where Hispanics and Blacks were the exception, and, when present, at least very wealthy.

"Not only is the governor dead, his daughter is missing," the senator announced. "And now a drug war has broken out in central Tucson. One cartel leader has been murdered on North Stone. Another, they think—not all the bodies have been identified yet—was gunned down near Grant and Campbell. A house got bombed. A cocaine house. People are dead from automatic weapons fire. Another explosive device hasn't gone off yet. Something big, the mayor tells me. Big enough to level a city block." The senator stood and stepped to the wall of glass that looked down over the Tucson valley.

"See that smoke?" he said. "That's where the bomb is. Should be spectacular when it blows."

Niki tried a piece of turkey, then spit it into her napkin. "Maybe we should go get some burgers," she whispered to her brother.

Their mother heard. She rose and marched unsteadily from the table to her bedroom, slamming the door behind her.

Brad shrugged. The senator never turned from the window. "Get me something, too," he said, never looking away from where Tucson's bomb squad might be momentarily vaporized. "Super-size, and with some of those seasoned fries."

◇◇◇

When the hole was big enough, Mad Dog poked his head out. The bad guys weren't waiting to grab them. A wall stood a few feet away—adobe or an expensive effort to look like adobe. To the right were clumps of brush, thick and high enough to block his view of anything but the tops of some nearby mesquites. To his left lay distant mountains.

He went back to work on the hole. Every effort made a lot of noise. Mad Dog expected the bad guys to burst through the door any minute. He paused long enough to stack up a bunch of grain bags in front of the door. Not enough to stop them, but enough to give him a warning.

The hole was already big enough for Cassie now, but he didn't think she should try to get away on her own. One last super effort should make it big enough for him, too. If that brought the men with their cattle prod, maybe he could put up a fight at the door. At least give the girl a head start.

But the bags proved unnecessary. He soon had a hole big enough even for a hefty Cheyenne shaman. He followed Cassie through with room to spare.

Mad Dog had brought a bailing hook and the pitchfork with him. Not the ideal weapons to counter what these guys were probably carrying, but they made him feel better. Mad Dog ducked down against the adobe wall and considered their options. There was a driveway and a cleared field to the west, toward those mountains. The brush to the east offered better concealment, so Mad Dog led them that way.

When they got to the end of the building, he dropped to his hands and knees, below the top of the scrub. Cassie did the same, and the two of them crawled through a tired screen of desert broom, creosote, and prickly pear. An empty corral lay behind the building. And, where the wall ended, more brush. They angled into it, seeing no one. Hearing no one. Expecting excited yells and the baying of bloodhounds that did not come.

Mad Dog and the girl bled from dozens of tiny scratches where thorns and brambles made it clear their passage wasn't welcome. Finally, they came to a place where the brush thinned. A row of mesquites grew along one of the many arroyos that crisscrossed the desert.

"Down here," Mad Dog whispered. There had been no rain for weeks. The wash would be bone dry and should prove a perfect route.

Cassie nodded and followed him through the trees and over the lip of the arroyo. It wasn't deep, but its sandy bottom was free of prickly vegetation. They could travel fast down here and stay out of sight.

Mad Dog checked behind them. Still no evidence their escape had been discovered. They had come quite a way northeast of the building in which they'd been held. For the first time, Mad Dog had a clear view of the house in front of the adobe wall.

"Damn!" he said. He recognized the place. And he recognized the mountains behind it. The house was an unlikely Santa Fe Ranch style and it stood half a mile from his trailer. He'd been kidnapped and brought practically back home. How crazy was that?

◇◇◇

There was hardly any traffic, and, what with everything going on today, Heather thought circumstances allowed for exceptions to the no-cell-while-driving rule. As she headed west on Ajo Way toward Three Points, Heather flipped open her phone and hit the speed dial to Mad Dog's place. A motorcycle ran a red light, making the reason not to multitask abundantly clear. It pulled out directly in front of her. Heather slammed on the brakes, lost hold of her cell, and nearly lost control of the Sewa patrol unit.

Even after she got the Toyota stopped, and scrambled to find her cell on the passenger's side floor mat, Mad Dog's phone was still ringing. Damn him for not having an answering machine. She tried his cell. It, too, rang and rang, then went to the message box he never checked.

She pulled the Toyota back onto the road. As she neared the turn off to her uncle's place, she felt an overpowering urge to take it. See if he might have gone back home and just wasn't answering the phone. But Captain Matus had been very specific about how urgently he wanted her and the letter she'd found returned to the reservation. She shook her head and decided to follow orders, this time.

Until she saw a wolf-like figure sitting in the middle of the highway right at Mad Dog's turn.

Heather tried to put flat spots on her patrol unit's off-road tires. The animal waited, confident, and she managed to stop just short of impact.

How like Hailey to come get her, Heather thought. But it wasn't Hailey. It wasn't even a wolf. A big German Shepherd, whose color and markings were similar to Hailey's, got up and trotted off the road. Disappeared in the nearby scrub in the direction of Mad Dog's place.

Heather would have followed Hailey without hesitation. Hailey had a way of appearing and letting you know when help was needed. Mad Dog believed she was his guardian spirit, and Heather thought that was an accurate description of their relationship. But this hadn't been Hailey. Still, what were the chances…? Why would a dog just sit in the road right in front of her, just before she would pass the road to her uncle's place?

She took the turn. On the way, she tried Mad Dog's number again. He didn't pick up, but she had a feeling she would find Mad Dog there. And trouble.

◇◇◇

Mrs. Kraus was on the verge of trying to sneak out a call again when the Benteen County Sheriff's Office phone rang. Ned caught her before she could get it. The phone rang a dozen times and then went silent.

"Who were you trying to call, Mrs. Kraus?" Koestel demanded. "And who was that?"

Mrs. Kraus gave him a winning smile. "I thought I'd call Bertha and see if she'd come down to the café and cater us some sandwiches and pie and coffee. That incoming call? I have no idea. This phone is thirty or forty years old. Don't have no caller ID on it. If you'd let me answer, I could tell you. Now I can't."

"Isn't there some number you can dial to find out where the last incoming call came from?" Koestel asked.

Mrs. Kraus thought he was right, but she didn't tell them that. Ned Evans shrugged. "Don't know," he said, "but that idea about Bertha's sounds mighty good to me."

Before Koestel could react, another militia member stuck his head and shoulders, and what appeared to be an M4, in the door. "Doc Jones is here to set up our MASH unit. Where do you want him?"

"What?" Koestel said. "Who called him?"

The guy spread his hands and disappeared. Doc followed a medical gurney stacked with supplies into the office.

"Nettie Frost, that's who called me," Doc said. "Wally Wasserman put his pickup in the ditch in front of her house and she found him passed out behind the wheel. So she called me. Wally's not hurt bad. Some bruised ribs and a bloody nose. And a crushed finger. Caught it in the breach of the automatic weapon he was fooling with as he drove to town to join you boys. Crushing the finger's what caused him to pass out and go in the ditch. Wally tells me you're seizing local government, so I called his wife to come fetch him home and headed right over. Figured I should be in the same place as all the dead and wounded." Doc waved a hand at his gurney. "I brought a bunch of body bags. You want to check them out?"

"Body bags?" Ned Evans took a step back. "Why on earth would you bring body bags, Doc?"

Doc wrinkled his forehead, which was pretty wrinkled to begin with. "Surely you don't think you can take over a government building in the middle of America's war on terror and not have the U.S military slap you down hard and fast."

"We're saving the United States, not going to war with it," Koestel said.

"That why you're wearing that secessionist flag on your cap?" Doc asked. "Wally told me you boys are all upset over Englishman seizing guns. That you're sure he's got a team from Alcohol, Tobacco, and Firearms helping confiscate every weapon in the county. But any damn fool knows that's not true. Englishman broke up a quarrel this morning, isn't that right Mrs. Kraus?"

"Yup."

"By himself," Doc continued. "As usual. No outside help. Right?"

Mrs. Kraus confirmed that as well.

"That's not what we're hearing," Koestel countered. "And Crabtree said the sheriff never would have got his guns if it hadn't been for all those armed men backing Englishman up."

"Yeah," Ned Evans said. "And now Englishman has gone out to the Porters to seize their guns. Word is, shots were fired there. And nobody's answering their phone."

Doc shook his head. "Well, I don't know what Englishman is doing at the Porters, but if he wanted to confiscate guns, surely he would have come after one of you boys first. I know for a fact several citizens have now reported you to the military. Told them armed terrorists have seized this courthouse and are holding hostages." He nodded toward Mrs. Kraus. "I suspect a crack counter-terrorism squad is on the way to Benteen County right now. When they get here, I figure you boys will need these body bags, unless I can keep a few of you alive to be tried for treason."

Koestel went to the window and peered at the sky, as if expecting to see the black helicopters beginning to circle. Or paratroopers dropping through the clouds. Evans checked a different window. While their backs were turned, Mrs. Kraus raised her eyebrows. Doc shrugged. Confirmation, as far as she was concerned, that he'd just made up all the stuff about a military response. Doc pulled up the edge of a blanket on his gurney. Mrs. Kraus recognized the butt of Doc's twelve gauge.

"Maybe you boys should save us a lot of collateral damage and just surrender to Mrs. Kraus right now."

Evans appeared willing, but Koestel straightened his back and found some bold words.

"My little band might prove a good deal harder to take down than you think, Doc. The traitors who fill those body bags may be the ones who try to seize the guns God and our forefathers gave us the right to bear."

"Damn!" Mrs. Kraus said. "These fools really want to kill someone."

◇◇◇

The professional was finished. All manner of side effects from this artificial drug war might cause problems his clients were probably expecting him to deal with. But his contracts were completed now. He'd done what he'd promised. The war had started, and now it would run its own course. He was through helping it along. And he was through eliminating inconvenient politicians, even if flaying had proved especially enjoyable.

Now for party time, he thought. Now for Heather English. She'd had a lot of luck and help when she beat him. He'd arranged for her to have neither this time around. He knew what to expect from her. She was good. Very good. But he'd take her easily. Kill her, slowly he hoped, in a fashion his photographic memory could recall with delight whenever he wished.

The professional dropped the motorcycle's kickstand and stepped off the Japanese crotch rocket. The front door of a rural Santa Fe-style house in Three Points opened and a pair of men in camouflage uniforms came out to meet him. A third man followed. This one wore blue jeans, boots, a green-flannel shirt that matched his eyes, and a Western-cut corduroy sports coat.

All three men were armed. The uniforms carried military-style automatic rifles. The butts of semi-automatic pistols protruded from snap-open holsters on their belts. The man in the sports coat wore a traditional Western holster strapped low on his right side. You could imagine him stepping into the street to defend his honor with that rig. Maybe heading for an appointment with the Earps or Clantons. His weapon was a huge Smith & Wesson Model 500, chromed, with pearl handles.

"Fifty-caliber," the wanna-be gunfighter said, noticing the professional's glance.

The professional preferred to work with his hands. "Have Mad Dog and the girl escaped yet?" he asked.

"No. Still in the barn," the shootist said. "Not smart enough to discover we left them an unlocked door."

The professional nodded. It could be difficult to free yourself from the flex-cuffs their prisoners were wearing.

"Then it's time to send them a traitor. Someone who can be careful. Mad Dog may have arranged a trap for the first person to go through that door."

The man in the sports coat laughed. The professional knew him as Lancer. It was what the secret service had called President Kennedy. The professional assumed it was no coincidence. That the designation had been adopted because the guy was commander in chief of this militia. And maybe because he considered himself a lady's man. The professional didn't care because the man was the channel for the real money today's events would produce. Fifteen million, so far, wired to offshore banks. Drug money was big. Political money, in this case, was much bigger.

One of Lancer's troopers smiled. The other met the professional's eyes and snapped a nod. That was enough for the professional.

"Have they seen you?" the professional asked the serious one.

"No, sir."

Sir. That was a nice touch. "Then you do it. Let them out. Make sure Mad Dog knows how close to home he is."

"Yes, sir," the man snapped. He loped around the front of the house and down the drive toward the metal barn out back.

"You want to watch?" Lancer said. "I had one of the cameras monitoring the brood mare stalls shifted to cover the door. That's how we know they're still in there."

Lancer wasn't the man's real name. The professional wasn't supposed to know it, but he did, of course. A professional researched his clients as well as his targets, and always knew the motivations of the people he dealt with. In this case, the professional knew the electorate wouldn't be pleased to discover Lancer's militia role. And he knew Lancer thought the evil they were doing was for the country's greater good. The people behind Lancer, the ones who hadn't told Lancer what results they really expected, were known by the professional, too.

The professional accepted the invitation and followed the two remaining men into the house. They passed through a monstrous great room decorated in traditional Western kitsch—animal heads on the walls looking over Hereford-upholstered wagon-wheel furniture. Half a dozen "soldiers" crowded an office at the end of a hall. Some cleaned their weapons. Some drank coffee. None paid much attention to the screens showing views of empty stalls and a closed door.

"No horses?" the professional said.

"I hated not bringing some here," Lancer said. "But I've kept this place clean of anything personal, the way you suggested. We can be gone in minutes and the rental arrangement can't be traced back to me."

The professional watched the screen on which the soldier he'd picked approached a door. The man tapped it lightly. Opened his mouth and said something—no sound—then twisted the knob. The lights inside the room were on. These pretend soldiers hadn't kept as close an eye on their prisoners as they'd been instructed to. Of course, he'd known that would probably happen. And seen his opinion reinforced from the attitude he'd gotten out front and when he entered this room. He wondered if Lancer was right about how sterile and untraceable this place would be. No matter, he would disappear long before that could become a problem.

The soldier stepped into the room for a moment and came right back out. He looked straight into the camera. The professional could read his lips when he said, "They're gone." The man put his hands together and jerked them apart, as if ripping a cloth. Or tearing apart the seams of a metal building.

"What's that fool trying to tell us?" Lancer said.

"Your prisoners left by another route," the professional replied.

"That can't be," one of the men in camos said.

The professional ignored the foolish statement and turned to Lancer. "Time to send a team after them. And remember, I don't want Mad Dog hurt. Just frightened enough to call for help."

By now, the professional thought, that would be very specific help. By now, Mad Dog shouldn't trust anyone but family.

◇◇◇

Sheriff English drove a couple of miles toward town before he pulled over beside a little bridge spanning an unnamed stream. Half a mile north, the stream rose from a series of springs. The vegetation along its course was all brown and lifeless now. From spring through fall, though, this was a beautiful spot. As a boy he'd come here with friends. He remembered a beaver dam. And how good the cool water felt on a sweltering day when they'd taken a dip in a deep hole. The joy of it had slipped some when they spent the next hour removing leeches.

The sheriff drew his pistol and examined it. Before Mrs. Walker's episode at the church this morning, he hadn't fired it in ages. The old Smith & Wesson .38 Police Special contained five cartridges, as usual, an empty chamber under the hammer.

According to that message from Mrs. Kraus, men with automatic weapons waited for him at the courthouse. Maybe as many as ten. The Porters had speculated about the local militia's make up and how many people they thought might join in taking the building.

His .38 wasn't much of a match. He pulled an extra cartridge out of his ammunition pouch and fed a sixth round into the last chamber. And he tried to remember when he'd bought this ammunition. Seven years ago? Eight? He'd bought it because a couple of rounds hadn't fired when he was doing a little target practice with his daughters. When had that been? They'd been in high school. Could this ammunition be old enough for that to happen again? He shrugged. Against a host of automatic weapons, it probably wouldn't matter.

For some reason the sheriff found himself remembering an old movie—*High Noon*. Gary Cooper, Grace Kelly, Katy Jurado, Lloyd Bridges, Lon Chaney, Jr.—all dead now. Just like he would probably be if he went back to town to face the guns in the courthouse.

In the movie, Cooper played a marshal who was retiring so he could marry Kelly, a Quaker girl opposed to all violence. At the last moment, Cooper learned a killer seeking revenge on the town would arrive with his gang on the noon train. Cooper, feeling responsible for the town's safety, decided to stay and face the threat. Kelly wouldn't support him. Nor would the townspeople or his former deputy. They all refused to help. In the end, Cooper went out to face the bad guys alone before getting the fantasy ending. Somehow, Sheriff English doubted there'd be a fantasy ending for him. This was no movie.

Who could the sheriff ask for help? He'd served this community for most of his adult life. But who were his friends? He could count on Mrs. Kraus. Doc Jones, the county coroner, too. But Doc's skill was saving lives, not taking them. The sheriff's family would have rushed to his defense, but none of them were here. Judy had lost a terrible battle to cancer years ago. Their daughters were grown up and gone. His brother lived a thousand miles to the southwest, not that he'd be much help anyway. Mad Dog would probably approach the militiamen with flowers to stick in their gun barrels.

The sheriff still had one deputy, but the man was so incompetent the sheriff no longer allowed him to carry a weapon.

The deputy's father, a former chairman of the Benteen County Board of Supervisors, wasn't exactly a friend, but the man had risked his life alongside the sheriff before. Of course he was on a holiday cruise with his wife somewhere in the South Pacific.

Bottom line, the sheriff realized, he didn't have many real friends. He knew everybody in the county and they knew him. But they had a professional relationship. He issued occasional traffic tickets, broke up fights, and served them with legal documents. In spite of that, they liked him enough to re-elect him, term after term, but he couldn't think of a single person he could ask to put their life on the line in a situation like this. It was a lonely feeling.

Like Cooper, he supposed, he had every reason to walk away. To let the community face the problem it wouldn't be willing to help him handle. But, when he took this job he took an oath. There wasn't any clause exempting him when he faced overwhelming odds.

The sheriff sighed. He had not the slightest idea of how to deal with this. But walking away didn't seem to be an option.

He put the Taurus back in drive and pointed it toward Buffalo Springs and the Benteen County Courthouse. He glanced at his watch. High noon had come and gone, but a lot more armament awaited him than Gary Cooper ever faced.

◇◇◇

Once Mad Dog realized where he and Cassie were, getting home was simple. Deciding whether to go there was something else. Whoever had kidnapped them must know where he lived. They could be at his trailer in minutes. And it wasn't like Mad Dog had anything there to use in defense. He didn't own any guns. Didn't want one, even now. He'd decided years ago he no longer wanted to kill things. He had a bow and arrows a Cheyenne friend had made for him. He had a baseball bat, a shovel, and an ax, and the hook and pitchfork he'd brought for "just in case." But he also had Hailey. That became his deciding factor. That and the availability of his home phone. He could hardly ask a young girl to disappear into the desert with him for a few days until all this blew over. And he couldn't let Pam come home from work into the middle of this mess.

Mad Dog followed the wash. It merged with a larger one, the arroyo that ran just west of his place. The sandy bottom was so churned up and soft that it made for hard walking. But there were also trails that wound among the trees—a few cottonwoods and lots of mesquite. Mad Dog often walked these trails with Hailey. He knew which ones would combine to take them home quickly, and keep him and Cassie hidden from the road.

The yard looked just the way Mad Dog had left it. He'd hoped to find it filled with squad cars, investigating the hand that had been delivered that morning.

No way. Not even any rolls of crime-scene tape indicating they'd been there. Instead, his yard was empty but for a cardinal taking a drink out of the tub he left by the front porch for Hailey. There was no sign of Hailey. Nor of the cardinal, as soon as Mad Dog and Cassie stepped onto the driveway that circled the tamarisk out front.

The front door was open. Mad Dog thought that meant Hailey had been the last in or out of the place. Opening doors didn't seem to be a problem for her. But, since she preferred them open, she tended to leave them that way. Even in winter.

Mad Dog bent and whispered in Cassie's ear.

"Wait here," he said, showing her a place to hide in the brush. "Let me make sure the coast is clear."

She nodded, burrowing into a clump of desert broom. Mad Dog trotted up the drive. He paused before mounting the porch. Listened. The cardinal scolded him from somewhere in the wash. A few other birds gossiped among themselves and Mad Dog wished he knew if they were talking about anyone following his trail. The double-wide was quiet. Mad Dog whistled a few notes of a favorite John Stewart song. Hailey usually greeted him whenever he'd been away from home. And she usually came for those notes, even when she was busy with something else. He half expected her to emerge from the front door, jump up and put her paws on his shoulders, and give him a thorough tongue lashing—in the literal sense.

Nothing. The tamarisk swayed in the breeze and the birds continued their conversation. No Hailey.

Mad Dog mounted the porch and cautiously stuck his head in the front door. There was no indication that anyone was there. No suspicious heavy breathing or sounds of guns being cocked. No bloody footprints. He stepped inside.

The possibility that someone waited for them was reason enough to leave Cassie in hiding. But Mad Dog also wanted to make sure she didn't see the hand. He didn't think it belonged to her missing father, but the girl had plenty of reasons to be traumatized already. The hand, however, no longer decorated his Christmas tree. Had the deputy found it? Not likely, not without crime tape all over the place. Maybe Captain Matus or Heather. Maybe the guy in the delivery truck had realized his mistake and come and taken the hand back. Maybe Hailey had hidden it. Maybe he'd even imagined the whole thing—the hand, Anjelica Grijalva, the kidnapping, Cassie….

He left the pitchfork and the baling hook in the living room and grabbed one of the house phones out of its charger. He stepped out on the front porch, waved Cassie in. She proved real by emerging from the bushes and running to join him. He dialed Heather as he led Cassie inside.

"Uncle Mad Dog," his niece answered. "Where are you?"

"Home," he said. He could hear a vehicle coming. Fast. He slammed the front door. Wondered if he had time to get to the pitchfork and hook. Decided he didn't and opened a closet, searching for his baseball bat. "I need your help and I need it now." The vehicle slowed and pulled into his front yard. "How soon can you get here?"

Footsteps mounted the porch. The only thing he could find in the closet was Pam's umbrella. A short, collapsible one with about the same ability to damage bad guys as a feather duster.

The front door flew open and Mad Dog threw himself out of the closet, umbrella raised, prepared to seriously muss someone's hair.

"Is this soon enough?" Heather said, both on his phone and from where she stood in the door safely beyond the umbrella's reach.

He heard another vehicle coming down the road. From the opposite way this time. From the direction of that Santa Fe house.

"I hope so," Mad Dog said.

◇◇◇

It wasn't part of his plan, but the sheriff went by his house on the way to the courthouse. Actually, he still had no plan. That was the problem. He knew he should call for outside help from the state. KBI or Highway Patrol. But outside help was exactly what the men in the courthouse expected. Outside help was almost certain to start an all-out war. However angry he might be at the men who'd seized his courthouse, they were people he knew. Just a collection of frustrated farmers who worked their tails off in a system that never seemed to make them a profit. He didn't want to get them killed.

His house was a more comfortable place to try to come up with a plan. Warmer, anyway. And he had a shotgun at home. His mother's old twelve gauge. A Remington Model 11 semi-automatic, almost a century old. She'd supplemented their larder with duck, geese, pheasant, quail, and the occasional deer. That's why he'd also inherited a nearly full box of rifled slugs—for the deer hunting. But talk about aged and questionable ammunition.

The English house was on Cherry, near the east side of town. It wasn't visible from the courthouse. Well, his roof could be seen from atop the courthouse's rickety tower, but that was all.

The sheriff parked on the street and let himself in through the unlocked front door. It occurred to him, as he turned the knob, that this might be the day he'd regret failing to lock up when he left. The house was empty, though. None of the militia from the courthouse had dropped by to take over his home. The place was as quiet and empty as usual these days.

The sheriff sat in the easy chair Judy had gotten for him soon after they were married the first time. It had taken one divorce and a second try to get their marriage right. He put his feet up on the ottoman. Her wingback stood on the other side of the end table that held their reading light. The novel she'd started the last time she sat there lay on the table, bookmark in place. Between pages twelve and thirteen of Harper Lee's *To Kill a Mockingbird*. An old favorite that Judy had tried to lose herself in. The chemotherapy and the cancer had made that impossible. Judy hadn't been able to concentrate. And so she'd picked the book up and started it, over and over, until she couldn't pick it up at all.

Their daughters found the idea of leaving the book on the table morbid. So they'd shelved it. But they were mostly away at school by then. The sheriff just took it back down and put it on the table as soon as they were away. Eventually, they'd left it alone. The sheriff had read it several times since, always carefully returning Judy's bookmark to the proper spot.

The sheriff unconsciously put a hand on the book. Seeking Judy's advice, or just some reminder of her. She'd had a mind of her own and a tendency to speak it. Hard to live with. Harder still to live without.

There was a phone on the table, too. As well as the remote for the old TV that sat across the room. The sheriff briefly considered calling his daughters. Saying goodbye. No, he decided. He didn't want them remembering him that way. He didn't want his last words to be false assurances of his well-being. He'd talked to both of them yesterday. And both were busy today, and not expecting calls. They knew him too well. They'd hear trouble in his voice. Better, if he died today, that they remember yesterday's conversations than whatever maudlin thoughts he might mumble on this Christmas afternoon.

He thought, too, about calling Mad Dog. The sheriff hadn't spoken to his brother for a week. He'd planned a call tonight, after Pam got home from work at the casino. Mad Dog might have a useful insight or—he smiled—a way to make things worse. The sheriff looked at the phone for a moment and then got up and walked over to the fireplace. The mantel was lined with photographs of his daughters. And Judy. He picked them up, one at a time, and remembered how much fuller his life had seemed when each was taken. They were a little dusty. He wasn't a skilled housekeeper. He started for the kitchen to find a dust rag. Half way across the living room, he stopped, disgusted at himself.

He was the sheriff of Benteen County, Kansas. If trouble waited for him at the courthouse, he had no business wandering around home looking at old photos and indulging in self-pity. He had a job to do. Even if he had no idea how to do it.

He turned and went back out the front door. Left the dust cloth untouched. Left the shotgun in the closet upstairs. Left the dust where it lay. Where, after his ashes were scattered on the Kansas wind, his own dust might join it.

A cold wind slapped him in the face as he stepped into the yard. A door at the end of the street opened. Mrs. Walker, whose Torino he'd shot out from under her that morning, stepped onto her front porch. She pointed a wrinkled arm at him. Made a pistol out of her hand, dropped her thumb like a hammer on a round, and jerked her fist up with simulated recoil. She blew imaginary smoke from her finger, turned, and went back inside her house.

All things considered, English decided, he'd be lucky to survive his trip to the courthouse before getting gunned down.

◇◇◇

Heather turned in Mad Dog's doorway and faced out into his yard. A black Jeep Wrangler swung into Mad Dog's drive. Top down. Four men tumbled out, all in uniforms and all carrying automatic rifles.

"Is the army after you?" she asked her uncle.

"That's not the army," Mad Dog said. "Not ours, anyway. Cassie and I just escaped from those guys."

One of the men stationed himself on the other side of the Jeep and drew a bead on Heather and the doorway. The other men scrambled. Two left, one right. Heather threw herself to the side, drew her gun, and checked their progress from the living room window.

"Police officer," she shouted. "Identify yourselves." In a lower voice she asked her uncle, "Who's Cassie?"

"Cassie Hyde," he said. "The governor's daughter. These guys kidnapped her and her dad last night. And they grabbed me today. I think they've got me confused with someone else."

A girl in jeans and a pony tail peered around Mad Dog.

"You're the governor's daughter?" Heather said. "Really?" How on earth had Mad Dog gotten himself involved in Arizona's crime of the century? And why wasn't she surprised?

"Yes, ma'am," the girl said.

Heather didn't have time for introductions. Or, thank goodness, for telling the girl what had happened to her father.

"Drop your weapons," she shouted. "Come out in the open with your hands raised."

No reply.

"If they start shooting," she told Mad Dog, "the walls of this place are going to offer about as much protection as cardboard. You two need to get behind something solid."

"I can put her in the closet behind my file cabinets. There's a heavy dresser on one side, washer and dryer on the other. It's not perfect, but...."

"Both of you, go there now." She tossed Mad Dog her cell. "Call Captain Matus. He's at a new number. My last outgoing call before I tried you. Tell him our situation. Tell him Cassie's here and we need help right now."

"I'll put the girl there, then...."

"No! You can't help me out here. Hide and use the phone. Leave this part to me. At least I'm armed."

Like her SIG was a match for the weapons that surrounded them.

"Drop those guns. And I mean now," she yelled. They didn't. And she'd lost track of the three who hadn't stayed by the Jeep. At least they weren't shooting. Yet. And they hadn't tried to enter Mad Dog's place so far.

"Are you Sewa Tribal Police Officer Heather English?" It was the guy behind the Jeep. How did he know her name?

"I am," she replied. "Who are you?"

"Someone will be here right away to answer your questions."

"Well, they can speak directly to the SWAT team that's coming any minute. I suggest you lay down your arms because they'll come in expecting trouble."

That was a gross exaggeration, she knew. If she was lucky, Mad Dog was on the line to Captain Matus right now. She wasn't sure the Pima County Sheriff's Office would send anyone. Not unless Matus could persuade them. If he couldn't, she thought Matus would send some of her fellow officers. But that would take time. Maybe twenty minutes.

"There's one out back in the mesquites," Mad Dog said from the door to the kitchen. "And one on this side, behind the tool shed."

"I told you to stay with the girl."

Mad Dog waved the phone at Heather. "Matus says the county doesn't believe him. But he's bringing every Sewa officer he's got."

It was what she'd been afraid of. But if Matus was coming, he'd come like the wind. Twenty minutes, maybe only fifteen.

She must have said some of that out loud because Mad Dog told her, "Don't worry. I'll help."

Great! An aging hippie pacifist who didn't believe in violence was going to help her hold off four soldiers with the latest in military weapons. And the bad guys were getting reinforcements. A motorcycle and a truck pulled up behind the Jeep.

"We need a miracle," Heather whispered.

Mad Dog nodded. He squatted down on the kitchen floor. Assumed the lotus position, except he couldn't get his feet up on his thighs.

"I'll see if I can manage one," he said. And then he threw his head back and began to whistle. Five notes. Over and over.

She recognized them. And wondered if he might not deliver. And if even that would be enough.

◇◇◇

Mrs. Kraus helped Doc set up his triage in the courthouse foyer. Doc wanted it where as many militia members as possible would see it. After getting chewed out by his commandant, Ned Evans had completely taken over her phones. Mrs. Kraus thought she might be able to get another message out through War of Worldcraft, but should she risk it? Englishman had been warned. He could get his own help. And stay away until it got here. That should be enough.

The militia had one man on the entry doors. One down the hall at the rear exit. One in the sheriff's office windows, and Ned Evans on the phones. She and Doc were trying to locate the rest. They had two guns at this little army's back now. They might make a difference if any real shooting started, but they needed to know where the other soldiers had stationed themselves. Judging from the way Koestel kept going up and down the stairs and checking with the guys on the main floor, at least one more gun must be up in a courtroom. Or maybe in the cupola, though the stairs that led up there had been blocked off for years. Unsafe, the county supervisors had decided, and too expensive to repair.

Doc made a show out of setting up tools like his bone saws and chest spreaders. Mrs. Kraus managed to slip behind the main staircase and go back into the jail. She'd thought she might pick a weapon or two out of Don Crabtree's arsenal—the one Englishman had locked up back there. Taking those firearms had apparently set these gun nuts off. Now they had seized local government in response to a threat that didn't exist. She had a copy of the key to the padlock on the cell. Only there weren't any guns in there anymore. Someone had cut the padlocked chain that secured it. The key to the original lock had been lost decades ago.

"Who stole Crabtree's munitions?" she demanded of Koestel when he next passed through the lobby on his circuit of inspections. "They're private property, in the temporary custody of the sheriff's department." Her outrage over the missing weapons outweighed the wisdom of letting Koestel know she'd been snooping. That she was a security problem he just might have to do something about.

"Why, no one stole them, Mrs. Kraus. We're not common thieves."

"Hardly common," Doc muttered, "this being the first time I recall anyone stealing a whole government building in Benteen County."

Koestel spun on Doc. "We haven't stolen this building. We're simply occupying it in order to prevent the powers that be from committing unconstitutional acts. People will call us patriots, not thieves."

"Fools," Doc countered, flexing the jaws on his rib cutters. "Dead fools, most likely."

"What about the guns?" Mrs. Kraus demanded.

"Why, Don Crabtree came and retrieved his property. Brought his own bolt cutters because we told him how they were locked up."

Mrs. Kraus' jaw dropped. "Sweet Jesus! That nincompoop is probably shooting up the Conrad place this very minute."

"Why would he do that?" Koestel seemed genuinely puzzled.

"Because that's why Crabtree's daughter gave us the guns in the first place. To keep her father from murdering the Conrad boys because he thinks they peed on his Christmas decorations."

"I didn't know," Koestel said, "or I wouldn't have let him take them."

"Which may make you an accessory to murder," Mrs Kraus said. "You and your whole damn army. And a total idiot. You took over this building because Englishman did exactly what you've just said you'd do under the same circumstances."

"Maybe your forces would be better deployed as peacekeepers over on Plum Street between the Crabtrees and the Conrads," Doc said.

Koestel looked like he was considering it. Then an automatic weapon chattered its way through a full clip. Nearby and from the direction of Crabtree's and Conrad's. Koestel threw himself to the floor and quick crawled to the nearest window. Knocked the glass out with the butt of his rifle.

"You're gonna pay for that window, buster," Mrs. Kraus said. But she was afraid Conrad, or maybe Englishman, might have just paid a whole lot more for no good reason on God's earth.

◇◇◇

After his little confrontation with Mrs. Walker, the sheriff had gone back in the house and traded his cane for his shotgun. When he left again, he went out the back door. The loose boards in his back fence hadn't repaired themselves. He slipped through into the alley and turned west toward Veteran's Memorial Park and the courthouse. Still without a plan, except he had something that threw bigger slugs than theirs. If his ammo was still any good.

The alley contained a few tire tracks, but its coating of dirty snow remained mostly undisturbed. His house was on Cherry, the street that marked the north border of the park as well as the courthouse grounds. The alley ran between Cherry and Plum, and Plum was where Don Crabtree lived across from Roy Conrad. Being in no hurry to die, the sheriff decided to follow the alley behind Conrad's place. That way he could take a quick look to be sure the warring factions were behaving themselves and no outbreak of violence seemed imminent.

Everything appeared calm enough from behind the Conrads. Their place had a high board fence, much like the one at the back of the sheriff's yard, though in better repair. Behind the house next door, though, the boards were older, weathered. A few hung askew, leaving gaps wide enough to peek through. Wide enough to crawl through, too, which tracks in the snow clearly indicated someone had done. The sheriff dropped to his knees and peered inside the adjacent yard. Just over the top of a classic Chevelle SS 396 parked beside the house, the sheriff could see half of Crabtree's home. And he could see the trail of the crawler, winding through raggedy evergreens, headed toward the fence that separated this place from the Conrads.

Why would someone crawl through the snow to the back of the Conrad's property? The sheriff could think of only one reason, and one person, foolish enough to do that just now—Don Crabtree. Especially if Crabtree had gone by the courthouse and liberated his arsenal. The sheriff took another look at Crabtree's house, hoping to see that Don had remained at home and at peace. As English looked, someone came to the window over Crabtree's garage. Crabtree's daughter—it was easy to tell because she still wore the same oversize sweatshirt. She stepped right up to the window. She seemed to be staring directly at the sheriff. Odd. He didn't think he'd be visible to her back here. He was still hidden by the fence he was considering crawling though. Looking at her father, maybe?

The sheriff became instantly convinced otherwise when she flashed a big smile and then flashed the rest of herself, pulling the hem of her sweatshirt up over her head. She wore nothing underneath.

A light bulb came on in the sheriff's head. This property belonged to Matt Yoder, a bachelor, living off the estate of his hard-working Mennonite-farmer-parents. Rumor had him as Buffalo Spring's most notorious womanizer. The sheriff hadn't thought of Yoder in connection with the Crabtree girl's late-night shenanigans. Yoder was way too old for her, at least in the sheriff's mind. Apparently not in Matt Yoder's or young Miss Crabtree's.

The sweatshirt came back down. The girl waved, definitely not at the sheriff, and grinned, and then turned around and lifted the hem for a different view. She might be a little girl to the sheriff, but she definitely had a grown up body. She scampered away from the window and picked up her cell phone. The sheriff heard a phone begin ringing in Yoder's house. He thought he should go have a chat with the man. Pass on a little wisdom regarding the age of consent and the penalties for statutory rape. But there was that trail through the evergreens. The sheriff had a bad feeling about it, especially if the Crabtree girl was sexting from her window instead of keeping an eye on her dad.

The sheriff's bad leg protested as he crawled through the fence and followed the trail. It was hard work, and difficult to keep the barrel of the shotgun free of dirt and snow. Worth the trouble, though, when he discovered Don Crabtree lying prone, Uzi to his shoulder, barrel poking through a slat in the direction of Conrad's home.

If the sheriff rushed Crabtree, the man would have time to swing the gun around and cut him in half. So the sheriff continued crawling. He slid forward, shoved the shotgun barrel up against Crabtree's butt, and said, "Drop it" in his most authoritative voice.

The sheriff evidently caught Crabtree by surprise. He yelped when the shotgun touched him, though you could hardly hear it over the string of explosions as the Uzi emptied its clip.

◇◇◇

"That voice sounds familiar," Uncle Mad Dog said. The voice in question had just called Heather's name. Heather had to agree. It did sound familiar, though she tried to deny it as she peered around the curtains into the front yard.

It was the guy who'd arrived on the motorcycle. One of those all-too-fast-for-a-human-to-control Japanese super bikes. The rider advanced on the house, taking off his helmet.

"Heather English," he called again. "Come out. Let's settle our business so everyone else can go on with their holiday plans."

He was small and compact and moved with the grace of a big cat. All that was familiar, too. Though when the helmet came off and she could see his face, it didn't match the man she remembered. But it had to be him. And, if it was, the rest of this crazy day began to make a twisted kind of sense.

"Heather," he called again. "Come on. No one will shoot you. You know you can trust me. Have I ever lied to you?"

Nightmare in Three Points. When she'd first come to Tucson, she'd visited the Yaqui Easter ceremonies, known her uncle would be crazy about them, and emailed him. Mad Dog immediately threw things in his car and drove a thousand miles. Minutes after arriving, he'd been accused of killing a cop. He ran, and soon it seemed the police wanted to kill Mad Dog instead of catch him. She'd searched for him, tried to help. And found herself the target of a mad man—the one who'd just reappeared in her uncle's yard, asking her to come out and play.

But for a lot of luck, the psycho would have killed her then. He was a professional hit man, and she had become a contract he intended to fill. Would have, if his employer hadn't double-crossed him. In the end, Heather had been responsible for letting the psycho escape. Not because he didn't deserve the most extreme penalties the law allowed. But because, in taking revenge on his employer, he'd saved Mad Dog's life. Now here he was again, striding across Mad Dog's yard. Telling her she was unfinished business.

"It's him, isn't it?" Mad Dog said. "That guy from three years ago."

"Yes," Heather said. "Stay with the girl. Let me see what he wants." Though, of course, she already knew. Because she'd been able to defend herself when he hadn't expected it, he'd developed a fantasy about her. Decided she could become a worthy test for his skills.

Well, she was good. Very good. Her father had taught her the self-defense techniques he'd learned in the military. Then, when her mother's illness worsened, she'd managed to find a little core of peace in the spiritual aspects of martial arts, and the exhaustion of the workouts. But she knew her limits. He was an expert. If they fought the way the psycho wanted, she was dead meat. To beat him, she'd have to cheat. Out psych him. Do something unexpected.

Heather holstered her SIG, leaving the strap unsnapped in case she had a chance to draw on him. She straightened her uniform and stepped to the front door. She took a deep breath, centered herself, and walked outside.

"Hello," she said from the porch. "I didn't expect to see you again."

He smiled. "I told you I'd be back. I told you I was back in that letter I left for you this morning. Didn't you believe me?"

"Sure. But a girl can hope."

The psycho tossed his helmet aside and peeled off his leather jacket. "Hope springs eternal."

"Yes," Heather said. "Yours, too, apparently. And not all your wishes come true."

The psycho smiled and nodded, as if to concede she'd scored a point there.

"What do you want here?" Mad Dog called from the door behind her. "We let you live."

Heather didn't take her eyes off the psycho. He nodded again, approvingly.

"True," the little man said. "But not a wise decision."

"He wants to kill me," Heather said. "This little fruitcake thinks I'm superwoman. Thinks it'll make him a bigger man if he takes me down."

"Why, yes, that pretty well sums it up," the psycho said. "Though, if the insults are supposed to spoil my focus and make me angry, they won't work. In any case, they're beneath you."

"Going to be all kinds of cops here in a few minutes," Mad Dog said. "You don't have time for this."

"You contacted Matus, then," the psycho said. "Good for you. I've arranged a delay for him. Nothing major, but enough. We won't need long."

Heather thought he was right. She'd gone up against him before. His skill level was amazing. She thought about grabbing her SIG and just blowing him away. But she could feel the sights of those guns on her. The guy behind the Jeep still had his weapon centered on her chest.

"You'll never clear your holster." It was as if he'd read her mind. "Besides, I just want you. I'll leave Mad Dog and the girl unharmed if this doesn't turn into a gunfight."

Well, she *was* better now. And she didn't have the option of forfeiting.

"What do you have in mind?" she said. "Marquis of Queensbury rules, I presume?"

"You can't do this," Mad Dog protested, though whether he spoke to Heather or the psycho wasn't clear.

"Free style. Hands, feet, whatever, but no weapons," he said, and shrugged. "And to the death of course."

"Of course." She slipped her jacket off and unbuckled her holster. Dropped her gun to the ground where she just might be able to get back to it. "But if this is going to be a fair test of your manhood, why not send these soldier boys home? It should be just the two of us."

"They won't interfere. They're just here to make sure no one else interferes, either. They'll leave when we're done. They won't harm Mad Dog or the girl. Or you, if you survive. You have my word."

"I'd rather have a beer," she said.

He smiled again. All her attempts to throw him off only seemed to confirm his opinion that she was the real deal. He obviously liked attitude. "You can have a beer afterwards, even if I have to pour it on your grave."

"Then let's do it," Heather said, sliding into a defensive stance. "I'm thirsty."

He matched her, then slipped to an offensive position. Karate, she thought. Or his own personal blend. She just tried to clear her mind of everything but him as she waited. She would either block him or she wouldn't. And she'd kill him as quick and dirty as she could, if the opportunity arose.

His eyes shifted to her side and she almost launched a strike. She held back at the last moment. He was just beyond her range and she suspected a trick. It wasn't, though. A growl penetrated her consciousness. Something big and silver gray advanced to her side. She didn't look down. She knew Hailey had joined her. Hailey had saved her the last time she met the psycho, but there hadn't been a small army pointing automatic weapons at them then.

"Want I should shoot the dog?" the man behind the Jeep asked.

"This noble creature is a wolf," the psycho said, "and of course not. Don't shoot her under any circumstances. She's part of this. I've been expecting her. But this time, I came prepared." He bounced back a couple of paces. "Bill," he called. "Now."

A man stood at the back of an old Ford pickup behind the Jeep. At the psycho's command, he opened the door on the box in its bed. Two massive pit bulls launched themselves from the truck like a pair of wolf-seeking missiles.

◇◇◇

Mad Dog watched the pit bulls rush Hailey. One was brindle. The other, liver and white. They were big, full-chested animals with the breed's traditional brick-like heads—all muscle and jaw. Eighty pounds each, at least.

Hailey crouched a little. Her thick hair came up around her neck and along the length of her spine. She was closer to a hundred pounds, though she looked bigger now. But to Mad Dog, she didn't look big enough to deal with this threat.

The pits must have smelled her from inside the truck. They were already salivating, spittle streaming from their mouths as if they were rabid. They threw themselves across the yard, eerie in their silence. No barking, no growls, just death on a mission.

Mad Dog watched Heather step toward the brindle's path. The psycho danced toward her and she had to sidestep, inter-rupting whatever she'd intended to do in Hailey's defense. Mad Dog came off the porch. Not that he had time to get to Hailey, let alone stave off either of the monsters.

In the instant before they arrived, Hailey leapt into the air—straight up. The beasts collided in the empty space where Hailey had been. One stumbled, hit the ground jaw first. The other, frustrated, buried teeth in his partner's shoulder. And then Hailey descended. She didn't go for either pit's throat. She caught the upright one by his hind leg. Slashed with saber-like fangs. Blood flew and the animal spun, suddenly awkward. The leg would no longer support him. He stumbled sideways, released his companion and pulled himself around to face Hailey. The liver and white recovered faster. And still had four good legs.

The psycho went for Heather. She blocked a hand strike, countered with a kick that missed and took a glancing blow to her ribs. Mad Dog knew it had to hurt.

Since the pits had spun about, Mad Dog was behind them. A couple of paces and there were some delicate targets he might kick. But the psycho was suddenly a whirlwind of punches, kicks, even a head butt. Heather fended them off, giving ground, seemingly just an instant too slow to counter every time. And growing slower. Mad Dog wondered if he should try to help her instead.

Mad Dog thought Hailey should be putting more distance between herself and the pits. She seemed to want to stay where she could protect her people. Or maybe not. A squirming little clump of fur emerged from beneath the trailer. Silver gray and teddy-bear plump, tottering on paws it would take some doing to grow into. Mad Dog couldn't believe it. A puppy? A wolf puppy? Hailey's?

Hailey sidestepped the liver and white and threw herself at the psycho. She didn't reach him, but she caught his attention and interrupted the flow of his attack on Heather. Heather took advantage of it to land an open handed blow to his sternum. It staggered him and seemed to give her confidence.

The brindle, too crippled to chase Hailey, noticed the puppy. The beast turned, went for it, moving faster than Mad Dog would have imagined a creature with only three legs could manage. Mad Dog kicked, caught the animal in the ribs, but hardly slowed it. Mad Dog started to throw himself onto the pit's back to protect the pup's tiny body. Something big and gray hit the brindle before it could reach its target. Not Hailey. She was still busy with the liver and white. A wolf, though, and a bigger one than Hailey.

A Mexican Gray. It took the brindle in the throat. The two of them rolled to the ground. Mad Dog grabbed the pup and turned in time to see Heather go down. The psycho held his side but advanced on her.

Sirens? Yes, Mad Dog heard sirens. The uniformed guy behind the Jeep must have heard them too. He shouted to his men to fall back. The ones on either side of the yard began backing away from the action. The one who'd gone behind the house suddenly sprinted around the corner. He didn't have his gun anymore. A pair of German Shepherds followed him. One savaged a piece of cloth as it ran. Something camouflaged.

The psycho stopped advancing on Heather as she bounced to her feet and resumed a defensive position. The psycho looked confused. He pointed at the German Shepherds.

"Shoot them," he said.

The uniform at the Jeep had gotten behind its wheel. The engine roared to life. The uniform on Mad Dog's left cried out. When Mad Dog looked his way, the man hot footed it for the Jeep, just behind the one from out back. The guy on Mad Dog's left didn't have his gun anymore, either. A huge Great Dane mix from down the road gnawed the gun's stock. A pair of Malamutes from half a mile north suddenly appeared from the brush behind the last gunman. He swung his weapon toward them but a normally friendly lab materialized from the brush to the man's right, teeth bared. The rumble from its chest sounding more like a promise than a threat. The man dropped his weapon and sprinted for the Jeep. Behind the Jeep, a boxer led a madly yelping Yorkie out of the trees. The liver and white pit backed away from Hailey. Its tail had been cropped, or it would have been tucked between its legs. The scrum between the second wolf and the brindle ended with the brindle crouched in fear. Trembling. Bleeding.

The soldiers made it to the Jeep as it backed over the motorcycle and into the road. The psycho reluctantly joined them. The guy who'd brought the pits had long since sought the safety of the cab of his truck. Ford and Jeep maneuvered around each other, surrounded by more dogs than Mad Dog had dreamed lived in Three Points. The Jeep bounced off a mesquite, then spun earth from under all four tires as the driver headed back toward the Santa Fe. The Ford followed close behind. So did the ill-matched dog pack.

"This isn't over," the psycho shouted.

Maybe not, Mad Dog thought, but score this round for the good guys.

Hailey approached Mad Dog, whined, took the pup gently in her mouth and set it on the ground where she and the big male wolf sniffed it from stem to stern to be sure it was all right.

"I thought I was dead," Heather said. "I thought we were all dead."

"Hey, it's Christmas," Mad Dog said. "We're supposed to get miracles."

◇◇◇

"Were those gunshots?" Doc Jones asked.

"Yeah, an Uzi," Koestel agreed.

Doc started to ask Koestel how he could tell, but Mrs. Kraus spoke first. "There was an Uzi in those guns you gave back to Don Crabtree, wasn't there?"

"Yeah," Koestel admitted. "But don't go jumpin' to conclusions. I got a couple of scouts out there. One of them's got an Uzi, too."

Doc pulled his medical bag off the bottom shelf of his gurney. "I'd better get over to the Conrads right away."

"No," Koestel said. "You're set up here. Let's wait. My boys'll report in. And this is the sheriff's office. We'll get calls telling us what happened and whether you're needed."

"Minutes might count."

Koestel pointed a gun in Doc's direction and snapped off a command. "I said, no, Doc. You can't help if those shots hit a human being. Thirty-two bullets in maybe five seconds.... You'll stay here until we know what's going on. Consider yourself drafted. You're now our official medical corps and, as such, under my command."

Doc would have argued but the phone began ringing in the sheriff's office. Ned Evans got the first line. Doc made it to the doorway as Mrs. Kraus got the second.

"Where?" Ned asked. Mrs. Kraus echoed him.

"This one just heard the shots," Ned told his commander, who, like Doc, was hanging his head through the doorway, waiting for solid information.

"Mine, too," Mrs. Kraus said, as both lines rang again.

The third and forth calls were just further reports of shots fired. But Evans exchanged whispered words with his next caller before announcing. "It was at Conrad's. No one hurt, though, and Englishman has arrested Don Crabtree."

"Damn," Commandant Koestel said. "That means Englishman's got Don's Uzi again." Koestel's cell chirped, interrupting any words he might have planned to share about how that made the sheriff a greater threat. Koestel stepped over into a corner where the continued ringing of the sheriff's phones drowned out his conversation. He was pale when he turned back to the room.

"That was one of our scouts. Not only has the sheriff seized Crabtree's guns, he's got himself a bunch of armed men with him over on Plum Street."

"Feds?" Ned wondered.

"Probably," Koestel said. "But locals, too. Our own neighbors, turning against us."

"You're kidding," Evans said.

"Time to stack your weapons and surrender the courthouse," Doc said.

Koestel shook his head. "Not hardly. This just turns it into a civil war. Friend against friend. Brother against brother. But that doesn't matter. We will do what we have to do. We will not suffer the tyranny of a government that seeks to disarm its citizens."

"What government would that be? One sheriff who hasn't been paid by Benteen County in months?" Doc asked.

Koestel didn't hear him. He'd turned to the window from which you could see the yellow flag with its "Don't tread on me" serpent. Koestel snapped to attention. Saluted. Doc noticed a single tear slide down the would-be patriot's face.

Zealot, Doc thought. This would get ugly.

◇◇◇

The sheriff was amazed. Don Crabtree had emptied a clip from the Uzi and every single bullet appeared to have been stopped by the RV Roy Conrad kept parked next to his garage. No one hurt. Not even when Conrad and his boys came running out of the house to defend it, all of them armed to the teeth.

If the sheriff were just an ordinary citizen, he would have ducked and called the sheriff's office when he heard shots. Most residents of Buffalo Springs had come running to see what was going on, instead. Several had taken the time to arm themselves. Most hadn't. A few said they'd called the sheriff's office first. A couple mentioned that some man had taken their calls, not Mrs. Kraus.

The rest of the Crabtree family joined the growing crowd early on. Edna and her daughter loudly blamed each other with accusations of, "I thought *you* were watching him."

Once they got beyond the recriminations, Edna asked the sheriff if she could take Don home for a change of clothes. His close encounter with the business end of the sheriff's shotgun had caused a little accident. The man really should have emptied his bladder before he went gunning for a neighbor. Roy Conrad was quick to point that out. The shame of the situation in which he found himself turned Crabtree into a meek prisoner.

The sheriff refused Edna's offer to take Don home. "He's under arrest, Mrs. Crabtree. Assault with a deadly weapon. Criminal damage—it'll cost thousands to repair that RV. Possession of a proscribed weapon. Maybe more. Depends on how many things the county attorney and I decide to charge him with."

Edna understood. "Can I at least get him some fresh clothes to wear while he spends the rest of Christmas in your jail?"

The sheriff said she could, but that raised a problem. He didn't have access to the jail.

"Oh, Daddy, how could you do a crazy thing like this?" Crabtree's daughter wailed. She still wore the sweatshirt the sheriff had seen through that window. At least she'd added a pair of jeans, though the sheriff would have wagered good money there was nothing under either but girl flesh. Under-aged girl flesh at that. He looked around and discovered Matt Yoder at the back of the crowd.

"Matt," the sheriff said. "I want to talk to you."

"Oh, sure, Sheriff," Yoder said. "I'll be happy to press trespassing charges against him if you want."

The sheriff let his gaze shift from Yoder to the Crabtree girl and back again. "That's not what I want to talk about," English said. Yoder and the girl both blushed bright enough to see in spite of the gathering dusk. "But now's not the time for that conversation. You ever finish your basement, Matt?"

"No. Why?"

"Larry Windor was a classmate of mine. We used to play ping pong in your basement when his folks lived here. I remember a bare concrete wall opposite the work bench. Just some pipes running along it. Stout enough I could maybe cuff my prisoner to one and leave him with you while I go take care of a problem at the courthouse."

"It's still like that down there," Yoder said. "Including the ping pong table."

Yoder, the sheriff noticed, had armed himself like most. But not with a fire arm. He had a heavy-duty sling shot in his back pocket. And lumps that might be smooth river stones. Add to that the old big-block Chevy by Yoder's house and the sheriff thought he'd just solved the second crime against yard decorations and that Yoder and he would be having quite a detailed conversation soon. If the sheriff survived the day.

"What's the problem at the courthouse?" someone asked.

English decided to tell them. He still wasn't sure how to deal with the men and the guns over there, but he had the makings of a pretty fair posse here. It seemed wise to find out if any of them were willing to help. Maybe he wasn't facing a Gary Cooper moment after all.

◇◇◇

The Sewa patrol units, three more Toyota Land Cruisers, came up the road from the east. Maybe, Heather thought, Matus had considered the possibility of the psycho arranging some way to delay them if they followed the usual route.

Captain Matus jumped out of the first Toyota. "You're all okay?"

Heather assured him they were, though she thought she'd be pretty sore later. None of the psycho's strikes had been solid, but more than a few had connected.

"They ran?"

Mad Dog stepped forward. "There's a big Santa Fe style house maybe half a mile west. That's where they were holding Cassie Hyde and me. That's probably where they've gone."

"The governor's daughter. She's here? She's safe?"

Cassie Hyde answered the question for herself by appearing on Mad Dog's front porch.

"Does she know?" Matus asked.

"Know what?" Mad Dog looked puzzled.

"Evidently not," Heather said.

"Shit!" Matus said. "Then I've got to tell her. We've kept it off the news so far, but that can't last much longer. She'll have to know before then."

Mad Dog scrunched up his forehead. "What are you two talking about?"

While Captain Matus grabbed a pair of his officers and hurried to join Cassie on the porch, Heather explained how she'd spent the first part of her morning. Cassie's quick flood of tears made it clear the Captain didn't have the time to be gentle with her. He left the girl clinging to one of the tribal policemen he'd assigned to look after her.

"Get your gun," Matus told Heather as he hurried across the yard. "Put on your vest." He turned to his other officers. "Pick up the weapons lying around this yard and get me a spare vest for this man. You're coming with us, Mad Dog. I need you to show us the place and identify suspects."

Someone handed Mad Dog a bulletproof vest that proved too small for him to fasten. Matus led the way to Heather's unit. "Heather, you know where we're going?"

She nodded.

"You drive, then. Mad Dog, get in the back. Get down on the floor when I tell you and stay there until I say otherwise." He turned to the officers with Cassie. "Take the last vehicle in our convoy. Get the girl out of here the back way. Take her straight to the county's Three Points substation.

"The rest of you, follow us. Weapons ready. We're going in fast, but that doesn't mean we're not going in cautious."

And that's what they did. They went, lights strobing, sirens howling. Heather led the column. She goosed the Land Cruiser down through the arroyo and up out of the trees that screened their view of the big house where Mad Dog said he and the girl had been held. She put her unit sideways, blocking a garage. She and Matus joined three officers on the front porch, one of them with a battering ram. It took him two tries to open the door, then they were inside, guns out, checking rooms, finding no one. Not even in the metal barn out back with the hole in a wall through which Mad Dog and the girl had escaped.

"That's the van they brought me here in," Mad Dog said, pointing at the UPS truck. Matus hadn't told Mad Dog he could leave Heather's patrol unit yet, but the Captain didn't seem surprised when Mad Dog joined them in the barn.

"And there aren't any other vehicles on the place," Mad Dog said. "Well, that's what I heard one of your people say."

A Sewa officer stuck his head in the barn. His normally swarthy complexion had turned unnaturally pale. "Basement in that house has a sound-proofed room," he said.

"What about it?" Matus said.

"It'll probably take DNA tests to prove it, sir, but I think we just found the rest of the governor.

◇◇◇

It didn't take long for English's posse idea to begin to pale.

"Actually, you know," one prospective member observed, "ammunition has been in mighty short supply since Obama got elected. That's why I stocked up, got three cases of .44 mags just the other day."

"Me, too," another agreed. "Been buying a box of ammo a week in case the federal government tries to disarm us that way instead of seizing our guns."

These men were creating their own shortages, the sheriff thought. And seemed quite likely to change their minds and support the bad guys in the courthouse when push came to shove.

"I sure do wish the President would come clean about his birth certificate," someone else said.

"The more I think about it," the sheriff said, "the more I think I should handle this alone. Too big a chance that some of you might get hurt."

"Don't be silly, Sheriff." The speaker was a Korean War vet. He carried an M1 Garand, the weapon he'd become familiar with sixty years ago. "We're glad to help. Besides, they won't shoot us. Most of us got invited to join them, I'll wager. I know I did."

Several people agreed. The sheriff decided he should have called in state law enforcement earlier. He started to reach for his cell but events took over.

"Why don't we go straighten this out," the old soldier said.

Someone handed the sheriff Don Crabtree's Uzi. "I stuck a fresh clip in. Safety's off. Just squeeze the trigger and this baby'll sweep a street clean of life, lickety split."

"Let's bring Crabtree," someone else suggested. "He can tell them what happened over here. Reassure them there ain't no government plot against Buffalo Springs. 'Sides, Englishman, he'll be right there when we take back the courthouse and you won't have to come back to get Don to put him in jail."

"If you're taking my Daddy," Crabtree's daughter said, "I'm coming too." So, it seemed, was pretty much everyone who'd gathered in Conrad's yard—about thirty people, maybe half of them armed.

"Lead on, Englishman," Roy Conrad said. "They take a shot at you, we'll clean their plows for them."

Conrad had a 20-gauge pump. If the sheriff marched his little army over to the nearest corner of Veteran's Memorial Park and began trying to shout out negotiations from there, Conrad's weapon might have the range to sprinkle bits of bird shot on the courthouse lawn once the shooting started. Plow cleaning was more likely to be accomplished by the guys in the courthouse with the automatic weapons.

"Hold on," the sheriff said.

No one did. Half a dozen people had already started walking toward the courthouse. The rest of the crowd followed, having given as much thought about what they were getting into as a herd of sheep following a Judas goat.

The sheriff could fire off a burst from the Uzi to get everyone's attention and then try to order them to stay here. Which, given the enthusiasm of those who'd taken up the point seemed unlikely to succeed. Or he could try and take the lead back. See if he could keep people from getting killed. Maybe even talk the band in the courthouse into surrendering. Or he could just resign, here and now, go pack his bags, and get in the car to spend a peaceful holiday season with his daughter and brother in Arizona. Even as he limped to the front of the crowd, he thought that last option had the most to be said for it.

◇◇◇

The militia at the courthouse had turned manic. They pushed around desks and chairs, building barricades across the front doors and behind windows.

"Bring those file cabinets from the sheriff's office," Koestel ordered.

"You will do no such thing," Mrs. Kraus said, crossing the foyer to stop them from moving her files by throwing her body in their path. Someone had opened one of the drawers. Pulled it out to make the cabinet lighter, easier to move, Mrs. Kraus thought. But the man was thumbing through files, not pulling other drawers. And he wasn't wearing a uniform or carrying a gun.

"Eldridge Beaumont," Mrs. Kraus said, "you know better than to get in our files."

Beaumont turned, looking suitably guilty. "I'm sorry, Mrs. Kraus. You were busy and the sheriff isn't here and I thought, under the circumstances, my client's files might be safer with me than…."

"Balderdash," Mrs. Kraus said. Eldridge Beaumont was one of two attorneys who actually lived in Buffalo Springs. And, it so happened, the man Englishman had told her would be suing the county on behalf of Mrs. Walker over the sheriff's disabling of her car that morning. "You have no right to even see those files until the county attorney decides which of them are relevant and constitute evidence in his case against your client."

"Well, technically that's true. But they're not in the hands of the county at the moment, so I thought I'd just have a peek."

"I am the county, and I'm still here," Mrs. Kraus said. "These bozos are trespassing, and we'll be taking care of that little problem directly. Now put that file back and get yourself out of here and…." She paused. "Say, how did you know they were in control here and how'd you get in?"

Beaumont's eyes searched the room seeking suitable answers.

"You in collusion with these terrorists?" Doc asked over Mrs. Kraus' shoulder.

"Something's happening across the park," someone shouted from the foyer.

"Lord, there's a bunch of them." That muffled voice drifted down from the second floor. "And they're armed."

Beaumont slipped past Doc and Mrs. Kraus and headed for the back door. He had the file with him.

"Hey!" Mrs. Kraus shouted at his back.

"I'll just be on my way. Won't trouble you anymore," the attorney called over his shoulder.

"Pick your targets," Koestel shouted, "and begin firing on three."

"Now just you wait a minute," Mrs. Kraus said.

"One," Koestel shouted. "Two,...."

◇◇◇

Captain Matus pulled Heather and Mad Dog aside. "That room in the basement is about to become the focus for the most intensive crime scene examination in Arizona history."

Heather didn't doubt it. Further examination had turned up a second corpse hidden under a drop cloth. That body had been preliminarily identified as "Quetz," the number two man to *Rabioso*, a drug lord murdered in central Tucson today. All by himself, and in light of what was going on, the one-handed Quetz was an important find. But since his remains had been only a few feet from a flayed corpse that was almost certainly the governor-elect of Arizona, you had to boost this from critical crime scene to one for the record books.

"The feds are on the way," Matus said. "So's the Pima County Medical Examiner. And one of the top forensic anthropologists in the country, a professor emeritus at the University of Arizona. He's coming out of retirement to join the investigation. Crime scene investigators from Arizona's Department of Public Safety will join them, as will representatives from every law enforcement agency with the necessary expertise or jurisdictional right of access. Real quick, now, there won't be room in that house for any Sewa participation. So I want you and Mad Dog to come with me to the Pima County substation in Three Points."

"Why?" Heather knew she had to straighten things out with the Pima County Sheriff's Office, but she couldn't imagine anyone she needed to talk to being available. Not now.

"I think Mad Dog can help with Cassie Hyde. And you need him to confirm your version of events. I don't think you realize how important the sheriff suddenly thinks you are. You found the governor's skin. You...."

Mad Dog's eyes got wide. Heather hadn't told him that part.

Matus didn't bother explaining. "The sheriff's office had Mad Dog's address flagged for false reporting. Then, the governor's daughter and the killer turn up there. And the governor's body, just down the road. Along with a corpse missing a hand."

"I don't suppose it helped," Heather said, "that I delivered his hand to the medical examiner's office."

"Caused quite a stir," Matus said.

"What should I have done?"

"You should have let me know, at least," Matus said. "By the way, did you know the guy you killed in that shootout in the junkyard was an expert taxidermist? A suddenly cash-rich taxidermist?"

Heather's jaw dropped. "You're kidding?"

Mad Dog, wide-eyed, shifted his head to follow the conversation like someone watching a tennis match for the first time, eye following the ball as he tried to puzzle out the rules.

"I'd need your gun and badge, because you should be off-duty pending an investigation into that shooting. But by the time the county responded, not only were you gone, so was Elvis. Lots of bullet holes. No corpse."

"What?" Heather said.

"You may rightfully imagine the sheriff has become tired of hearing your name. Especially since he ignored it when he should have responded and only came to believe you were for real after our contingent of Sewa Police confirmed the presence of the governor's daughter. At this point, the Pima County Sheriff isn't the only law enforcement officer in Arizona wondering whether you've been too conveniently where so much is happening.

"Today has gone completely off the map. You probably don't know an all-out drug war has broken out from Tucson down to the border. Oh, yeah, the sheriff very much wants to fit you into his day, Heather. In fact, he wants to see you now. I can't do anything else here because this place is being taken over by the big dogs, so I figure Mad Dog and I should come along and see if we can answer some questions. Maybe mitigate his response to you. Be there as witnesses if he wants to charge you as an accomplice."

"Oh," was all Heather could manage. Mad Dog's efforts to reassure her were interrupted when a marked Pima County Crown Vic entered the yard, tires throwing gravel, lights flashing star-spangled-banner colors. The Ford skidded to a stop beside the three of them and a pair of deputies scrambled out.

"Captain Matus," the one with the braid on his shoulders said. "We just found one of your Toyotas near the Three Points substation. It contained the two officers you sent to escort the governor's daughter to us. They're dead."

"Jesus!" Matus said. "What about the girl?"

"No sign of her." The man and his companion had their hands on the butts of their service weapons. "The sheriff said we should bring you and Officer English to him right now, sir. And not to take no for an answer."

◇◇◇

"Thr…," Koestel began. He didn't manage to finish, because Mrs. Kraus caught him with a roundhouse swing of her purse. Her Glock was in it, as were a cluster of keys, an overflowing coin purse, and a variety of other heavy objects. Some of them—a tin soldier depicting a World War I doughboy, for instance—she would have had difficulty explaining.

The militiaman in the adjacent foyer window looked at Mrs. Kraus in shock. Doc covered him with his shotgun, however, and the man dropped his weapon and put up his hands.

"Thr…," though it was unlikely to have been heard throughout the courthouse, had the assumptive effect of most rhythmic chants. A pair of automatic weapons began chattering. Short bursts. Soon, other guns lining the courthouse windows joined in.

"Damn!" Mrs. Kraus said.

Doc Jones might have added his own comment, but Ned Evans suddenly appeared in the door to the sheriff's office. Doc swiveled his shotgun to cover Ned and said, "Drop it."

Ned continued across the foyer, not dropping it. Walking straight toward Doc. "You won't shoot me, Doc," Ned said, "so just hand it over."

Mrs. Kraus clawed through the contents of her handbag, so recently rearranged by the collision with Commandant Koestel's cranium. She pulled out the Glock and aimed it at Ned. "Doc might not, but I will."

"No, you won't," Ned told her, "and since you've gone and assaulted our leader, I'm afraid I'm really going to have to take your gun away this time."

Mrs. Kraus noticed the man they'd just disarmed reaching for his own weapon. Apparently, he too had decided she and Doc weren't really threats. So she shot Ned in the knee

His weapon went off and stitched a series of holes in the foyer's scarred tile. A line directly between Doc and herself and uncomfortably close to both. Ned screamed. But at least the guy by the window threw his hands back up.

"You shot him." Doc seemed more than a little surprised. He dropped his shotgun, grabbed his medical bag off the gurney, and went to Ned's assistance. Mrs. Kraus was pleased to note that Doc proved wise enough to toss Ned's gun to her and get it out of the reach of any nearby militiamen before taking a pair of scissors to Ned's jeans. Mrs. Kraus didn't know how to shoot the fool thing so she shoved it under Doc's gurney. Out of sight, out of mind, she hoped.

Ned rocked back and forth on the floor and made moaning sounds as Mrs. Kraus ran over and retrieved another weapon from the man by the window. She got Koestel's as well, and put them under Doc's gurney, too. There was another gunman in the sheriff's office. One was in a nearby supervisor's office, from the sound of things, and at least two upstairs. Now what?

She didn't have time to think about what she'd done to Ned. The guy who'd been in the sheriff's office came around the door frame at floor level and threw a wild burst into the foyer. Mrs. Kraus sent three rounds back at him before she realized that fresh screaming sound in the foyer came from her own throat.

The floor rose up fast. It was covered with blood. Her blood? No one else was near enough to....

◇◇◇

Sheriff English remembered his mother telling him how the Benteen County Veteran's Memorial Park had been dedicated to future peace—that those who fought and died to preserve it should not have done so in vain. It was a square block, cut out of a prairie city that, aside from the creek winding along its west side, was not confined by natural boundaries nearer than the Rocky Mountains. City blocks here were of generous proportions, more than six hundred feet on a side. There was another forty feet of street between the courthouse and the park. And then the court building stood behind another eighty-odd feet of occasionally groomed lawn. So, as he and his running-itself posse came out from behind the buildings at Cherry and Adams, he estimated the nearest gun that began firing on them had to be about eight hundred feet away.

Sheriff English didn't know what kind of automatic weapons they were, but he remembered the effective range of the M16 he'd carried in Vietnam almost forty years ago was nine hundred feet.

"Take cover!" he shouted.

He followed his own advice, ducking back around the corner of a brick wall—part of what had been a dry cleaning establishment until sometime in the sixties. The effective range of his Smith & Wesson .38 Police Special with its four inch barrel was more like fifty feet. If he shot back from this distance, he *might* actually hit the courthouse someplace. But he wouldn't hit the guys shooting at him. No way.

His shotgun would do better. He had recovered it when Crabtree's Uzi proved unsatisfactory as a cane. But even with its rifled slugs, he'd need more luck than skill to hit a concealed shooter at this range.

The sheriff examined the situation from behind the wall of the former dry cleaner. Most of his "posse" had followed his suggestion. In fact, most of them had taken cover by turning around and running back east on Cherry. But several men returned fire. Some, at least, had dropped to prone positions in the shallow ditch at the edge of the park. But three stood in the middle of the street and snapped off shots as if they had just shouted "pull" and the danger to themselves equaled that from the average clay pigeon.

One of them was the Korean War veteran, who should know better. His M1 Garand seemed to be placing a nice pattern in one of the courthouse's second story windows. But, beside him, another man fired his twelve-gauge shotgun from the hip, racking his slide like some street-gang warrior. The only damage he did appeared to be substantial pruning of some nearby evergreens. Another guy with a .22 target rifle punched out a window in one of the supervisors' offices. The window had been closed, though, indicating no one had been shooting from there.

Just down the street to the south, a man wearing camouflage stood under one of the town's few working street lights with his cell phone in his hand. What looked like an assault weapon hung from one shoulder. He punched in a number, paying no attention to the whistle of passing bullets or the whine of occasional ricochets.

"You idiots, get down," the sheriff shouted.

The veteran trotted over and stood behind a tree at the edge of the park, though the girth of its trunk was only about half his size. "I can't get up or down so good these days," he called, resuming his marksmanship on open courthouse windows.

The guy with the shotgun ran out of shells and came back around the corner to join the sheriff. The one with the target rifle turned and scowled, but then joined the men shooting from the ditch. The one on the cell phone kept punching buttons until his cell flew in the air, his body crumpled to the street, and the back of his head followed the bullet that had just torn through his cranium and splattered the brick wall behind him next to a window containing a sign—EAT MORE BEEF.

"Jesus," the sheriff muttered. "Wasn't that Paul Graber?"

"Yeah," the guy with the shotgun said. "I noticed him down there on Jefferson. I wondered what he was doing out here. I heard he was on their side."

◇◇◇

Heather's meeting with the Pima County Sheriff didn't start well. First, the sheriff didn't want to see Mad Dog, and Mad Dog, who hadn't really wanted to come to the substation except to explain why his niece shouldn't be in trouble, did not quietly accept being kept out of the meeting. Even after the door closed on the office the sheriff was using, Heather heard Mad Dog demanding admittance. She hoped he wouldn't get himself arrested. But she wasn't sure she wouldn't be arrested, especially after Pima County Sheriff Johnny Behan demanded her weapon and badge the moment the door closed.

She didn't get a chance to respond to that. Captain Matus, who had refused to let her see the sheriff outside of his presence, told Behan he had no right to do that.

"Heather English is a Sewa officer under my direct supervision. She answers to me, not you."

Behan took that about as well as Heather expected, considering what she'd heard about the man. His quick temper and imperial manner had only been rumors until now. Like the stories of political deals and whispered hints of corruption.

Johnny Behan looked as slick as his campaign posters, except he smiled for those. He was short and compact and older than his shining even teeth and thick dark hair indicated. He was handsome, or he would have been if he hadn't been shouting insults about her competence and hinting that she had to be involved. Fortunately, Captain Matus proved inflexible in his defense of her.

"Well, damn it," Behan said, "if I can't relieve her from duty, I can by God arrest her."

Matus didn't have an immediate answer for that. Behan could arrest Heather. She knew, because she was a licensed attorney and a member of the state bar of Arizona. Behan could arrest pretty much anyone he wanted. Whether he could keep her in jail for long, or might even open himself to litigation for wrongful arrest, was another matter.

"Are you arresting me, sir?" Heather said into the brief silence.

"I'd say that's mighty likely," Behan snarled.

"Well," Heather said, "decide. I'm here willingly, as requested, to make a complete and formal report of my experiences today. But if you're arresting me, sheriff, then you need to know I'll assert my right to remain silent."

Everyone knew about their Miranda rights these days. But the Supreme Court had recently limited them. Suspects now had to inform an arresting officer that they intended to exercise their right to remain silent. No assumption of that right remained following the court's decision. A suspect who refused to speak at all could have anything they eventually said, even much later, used against them.

Not that Heather expected formal charges to be brought against her. She was just being bullied. And she thought her best defense against that was the one she'd just used. Behan might actually suspect she was implicated, since she'd been in the middle of so much of what had happened today. But when she explained her actions, the worst that could be made of them involved her competence as a law enforcement officer. For that, she was answerable to the Sewa Tribe and Captain Matus, not Pima County. Behan, she thought, wanted to know what she knew, even if it turned out that he already knew most of it.

"Little girl," Behan said, "do you have any idea how long I can make you disappear into the system?"

"Yes, sir." She did, because of her law degree, her studies, and because her father had occasionally used similar threats when he thought it was the only way to find out what he needed. "I believe I do. And, since I'm an attorney as well as a cop, I have a pretty good idea of what damages a jury might grant me for wrongful imprisonment. You might want to check with the Pima county attorney if you'd like an opinion on that figure, or with the county manager about how it could affect your budget."

Behan's glare should have burned her eyes out and caused the flesh to melt from her face. "I will remember this, Officer English. Don't think I won't."

"Does that mean you're not going to arrest me?"

"You want it in writing?"

"Yes," Heather said. "I think I do. Captain Matus can witness it. Then, with his permission, I'll give you my full report."

Matus let one corner of his mouth turn up in the tiniest of smiles.

Behan stepped to the door and shouted down the hall. "Bring me some letterhead stationery," he said. "And get someone in here to record a statement."

Heather heard a voice in the lobby. "You've got a wolf?"

"She's like a witch's familiar," her uncle said, "only completely different."

◇◇◇

Sheriff English peered around the corner of the brick wall to check on his little posse. There weren't many out there anymore. And, to his surprise, that was not because they'd all died. Instead, little by little, they'd run out of ammunition. At which point, continuing to lie in a shallow snow-filled ditch had become less attractive. Especially when that ditch was being raked with automatic weapons fire, plowing fresh rows that revealed the black earth beneath the snow. The same sod in which their coffins might soon rest. Once they ran out of ammunition and no longer had the fun of shooting at people to occupy their minds, the concept that someone was shooting back, trying to kill them, seemed to finally come clear.

"Out of ammo" or "gotta get more bullets" became the mantra of the men who'd retreated past the sheriff's spot into the neighborhood and fled into the darkness. So far, none of them had come back.

The sheriff had noticed faces appear at windows in the houses lining the north side of the park when the shooting started. Then blinds were drawn or curtains pulled. He didn't think that would keep the bullets out, but it was Christmas and not everyone wanted to interrupt their holiday.

To the sheriff's amazement, Paul Graber appeared to be the only casualty. The sheriff had wondered if he should run down the street to be sure Graber had truly left for that unexplored country. But the back of Graber's head was missing. Even from the corner behind the dry cleaners, it was clear the man must be dead.

Conrad was one of the few who paused at the corner when he abandoned the ditch. "Don't waste your life going for Graber," he said. "It's the old man who needs your help. His M1 is out of shells and he says his bad knee has seized up on him. Says it's time we should get him some fresh clips and evacuate him from that ditch. I'll handle the clips if you'll manage the evacuation."

"Sure," the sheriff said, thinking Conrad meant it as a joke, except Conrad immediately sprinted east toward his place and the vet's.

The sheriff peered around the corner again. Only the Korean vet remained, as far as he could see. It had gotten dark while the two sides exchanged fire, but all the other spots he remembered being filled by posse members were now vacant. No guns fired from his side of the park. Not much came from the other side. A moment after he pulled his head back, two short bursts ripped through an evergreen across the corner from the dry cleaner's. And then it was suddenly quiet.

"You need help?" the sheriff called to the vet.

"Not really. Think I got at least one of the guys downstairs. I'd just as soon wait on some fresh clips if you don't mind."

With his own bad leg and the vet's problem knee, the sheriff didn't think he could get the man out of harm's way without giving the bad guys a couple of hours of target practice. But he couldn't just leave the man there, either.

"Hello the courthouse," English shouted.

There was no immediate answer. No fresh rounds got sent his way, either. The sheriff decided that was a good sign.

He stepped out from behind the brick wall and called again. Not far out, in case he needed to dive for cover. He tried to look official, but not threatening. His pistol was holstered and he still had his shotgun, though he rested the butt on the street like the cane he should have brought instead.

"Hey, Englishman," a voice shouted. Good Lord, it was Doc. "Anybody over there need my services?"

"There's one beyond them," the sheriff yelled. "Otherwise, in spite of all the lead that's flown, we don't even have any wounded I know of."

"Good thing, 'cause we got several wounded over here. Some serious enough I'm trying to persuade their commander to let me call for help."

"Who's in charge? Let me speak to him."

Doc called back. "That would be Commandant Koestel, I suppose. He can't hear you at the moment on account of a ringing in his ears. Can't see too good, either. Double vision. Concussion, I'm guessing, though he's not hurt bad enough for me to have had time to check him out yet."

"Then who do I talk to?" The sheriff was surprised to find he'd crossed the street and now stood at the edge of the ditch in which his last posse member lay, unable to get up or offer supporting fire. At least, the sheriff told himself, no one was shooting at them.

After a moment, Doc called again. "The commandant wants to know if you're ready to surrender. I told him, considering how many of his people are dead and wounded, his question indicates a more serious brain injury than I originally suspected."

"Tell him the only dead man over here is Paul Graber. One of his, and shot by his own men. Ask him if he's ready to give up before this fiasco costs any more lives."

"No, the damn fool won't surrender. He says they'll fight to the death rather than betray their values."

"Well," English called. "Tell him I can't surrender, either. I can't let a band of fools seize our courthouse. That would make me a traitor to my duties and my nation. Tell him I'm coming over there so we can continue this conversation man to man. Surely we can find some rational way to end this situation without further loss of life."

The sheriff was already well into the park, and deep into his Gary Cooper moment when another burst of fire echoed from the courthouse. He stood still for a moment, taking stock of all his body parts and waiting for one to complain of serious injury. But he'd heard shots, not bullets. No whistle as they passed, no thuds of impact as they tore into flesh or the park's snowy surface.

"Don't shoot. I'm coming to talk," the sheriff shouted.

"Accident," Doc called. "I think you're safe to come on in."

The sheriff stepped around the remains of the old fountain and suddenly stood fully in the open. There were no more thick weeds or groves of evergreens to mask him from the courthouse windows. Several of those windows were open. More had been shot out. As he got closer, he could see that the brick façade bore many fresh scars. And that the yellow flag with its snake still flew from the flagpole in front of his office.

The sheriff detoured from his direct approach to the building's front doors. He went to the flagpole, untied the knot, and let the banner fall to the snow. Then, despite its bold motto, he made sure he stepped all over it before limping up the stairs to the entrance.

His heart was beating very fast and he found it hard to catch his breath. He managed, though, and after banging on the doors with the butt of his shotgun, called out, "Open in the name of the law."

A very pale Mrs. Kraus pushed the door open for him. Her blouse was blood soaked, as was a cloth bound to her forehead.

"Lordy, Englishman," she said. "Have you gone and succumbed to a testosterone rush like these fruit loops in here? Come on in. You know these doors don't lock."

◇◇◇

Though Heather had done what she could to insure she got out of the sheriff's substation, she was surprised when they actually released her. She had the sheriff's signed promise, but she'd been afraid he'd slide around it and hold her in protective custody. The man who had murdered the governor-elect of Arizona had a personal beef with her. He would probably come after her again. Now, if he could. Or soon, if things were too difficult at the moment, because every law enforcement officer in the state was looking for him.

Mad Dog had been given a ride home earlier. Once he was assured his niece wouldn't be arrested, he'd been eager to get back to Hailey and her pup.

As Matus started the Sewa patrol unit, he nodded across the parking lot. An unmarked sheriff's unit pulled out onto the road. Several other unmarked units sat in the lot, occupied.

"You know what Sheriff Behan is doing with me, right?" Heather said.

Matus nodded. "Bait."

"I'm the tethered goat. They're hoping he'll try for me again and they can grab him. Take him down"

"I don't think Behan gives a damn if you go down, too."

Heather thought he was right. "How many people do you think he's assigned to me?"

"Enough to follow us, and follow us by leading, though they must be sure I'll take you to your uncle's place, or back to the reservation. I'm guessing four cars and eight detectives, all together. Maybe more."

"If the psycho comes, they might not be enough."

"That's why I should stay with you myself," Matus said, "or take you back to the Rez and keep you there until we're sure this guy is gone."

Heather latched onto the "should" in that sentence. "But you're not going to do that."

"Well, I can't stay with you. We just lost two officers and I've got to break that news to their families. And I know you well enough to realize that taking you back probably won't work. You won't stay on the Rez because Mad Dog could still be at risk. So, I'm just going to drop you at Mad Dog's and hope you and Hailey and a bunch of the sheriff's people can keep things safe there."

Matus pulled out and headed toward Mad Dog's. A pair of unmarked but obvious law enforcement vehicles followed them out of the lot. A third also entered the street, but turned the other way.

Heather looked at her captain. "There's more, something you're not telling me."

"I think he's gone. I think your psycho is somewhere in Mexico by now. That's what happened the first time you and he met. When the wheels came off and Arizona law enforcement was issuing BOLOs all over the state, he headed for the border. But he took two runs at you before he went. I can't help but think he might have a backup plan for you. So I'll see if I can turn around and get back up here soon, or get you some help interested in keeping you alive as well as catching him."

"You won't have time. You're already shorthanded."

"I know. So play this smart. Stay with your uncle. Let those sheriff's deputies keep an eye on you. Spend a quiet evening with family. Help Mad Dog do some woo-woo magic stuff to foil this guy and get back to celebrating Christmas, okay?"

The captain's comment about celebrating Christmas reminded Heather she was supposed to be in the Tucson foothills to meet Brad's family in a couple of hours. Could she still do that? Would her traveling parade of sheriff's detectives be enough to keep them safe? And how would she get there? She didn't have a patrol unit anymore. Her car was down on the reservation.

The captain pulled into Mad Dog's yard. A trail of dust indicated another car had been down the road a few minutes before. One of those sheriff's units, probably. One of the cars that had followed them turned off at the corner before Mad Dog's. When they passed the big Santa-Fe house, its grounds were packed with more law enforcement vehicles. Maybe he wouldn't come for her here, Heather thought.

Mad Dog stepped onto his porch to greet them, Hailey at his heels. Mad Dog held a little ball of fur in his big hands. "It's a boy," Mad Dog said. "I've been considering names for him and I think I got the perfect one."

Matus rolled his eyes. "Jesus!" he said.

Mad Dog looked disappointed. "How'd you guess?"

◇◇◇

The foyer of the courthouse looked like a battle had been fought there. Which, the sheriff realized, wasn't surprising since that's exactly what had happened. Broken glass, shattered tile, bullet holes, and blood everywhere.

"Are you all right?" the sheriff asked Mrs. Kraus.

"Hurt myself more when I slipped than when that piece of shrapnel sliced open my forehead."

"When she fainted, she means," Doc said. "I really need to check her out more thoroughly, but...."

The reason for his hesitation was clear. As the sheriff watched, Doc cut away clothing from the blood-soaked boot of a man whose clenched teeth and pale features made clear his pain.

"How many dead?"

"Two," Mrs. Kraus said. "One from upstairs, and the pecker-wood who shot at me. I meant to wing him but caught him right between the eyes. And then this guy," she gestured at the man Doc was treating, "realized the other guy up there was dead and he came running down the stairs to see what Koestel intended to do about you. He tripped. Lost control of his weapon and blew some holes in his foot. Hardly any of this little army is unscathed. Just the two prisoners in the corner. I had to shoot Ned Evans in the knee. Koestel's not been shot, but I wholloped him over the noggin pretty good. You might want to arrest him while you got the chance."

Koestel looked up from the floor. Someone had stuffed a blanket under his head and he was unarmed. "Ah, sheriff, come to offer me your sword?"

Brave words, English decided, though less impressive since only one of Koestel's eyes managed to track the sheriff as he kneeled beside the man.

"You have the right to remain silent," the sheriff began. Then he looked around the room. So far, thanks to Doc's labors, five of them remained alive. "That goes for all of you," he said, before continuing to recite Miranda.

"You need handcuffs?" Mrs. Kraus asked.

"Please."

She reached into her purse and pulled out a role of duct tape. "We got no more cuffs that work," she said, "but this'll hold him.

"Ambulance is on the way," she continued. "I called when the guy Doc's cutting on stumbled down the stairs. By that time, everybody down here had been disarmed. Highway Patrol is coming, too, because you don't have the personnel or facilities to house so many criminals."

The sheriff realized he could see his breath in the glow of the foyer's neons. With all the windows that had been shot out, the courthouse's inadequate heating wasn't likely to keep it above freezing back in the jail. Not that most of these guys were fit enough to be kept back there, anyway.

"And, speaking of prisoners," Mrs. Kraus said, "what happened to Don Crabtree? I thought you captured him after he shot up the Conrad place?"

It was the first the sheriff had thought about Crabtree since he and his posse started for the courthouse. Someone had been herding Crabtree in this direction. The sheriff remembered seeing him as the crowd neared the corner, just before the shooting started. But not since.

"You need my help, Doc?" the sheriff asked.

"Not unless you've acquired an advanced medical degree I don't know about. Go get the son-of-a-bitch before he drums up more business for me."

The sheriff turned toward the door.

"Here," Mrs. Kraus said, handing English her keys. "Take my car. It's out back. Otherwise that leg of yours is gonna give out on you."

"Thanks," the sheriff said. "And I guess I'll take the duct tape, too, if you don't mind. In case Don has gotten out of the cuffs I put on him."

"Wouldn't need more than a paper clip for that," Mrs. Kraus said. It wasn't an exaggeration.

"And, while you're out there," Mrs. Kraus said, "you should have some words with Eldridge Beaumont, Mrs. Walker's attorney. He was in here in the middle of this mess, helping himself to her file. Like maybe he didn't expect you to be around to deal with charging her after today."

"Beaumont?" The sheriff remembered how Mrs. Walker had shot him with her finger as he left his house. "Say, isn't Mrs. Walker some relation to Don Crabtree?"

"Rich aunt," Mrs. Kraus said.

"My aunt, too," Koestel muttered. "And a true patriot, since she alerted us to your collusion with federal agents and your plan to seize our guns today."

That caught the sheriff by surprise. "Does he know what he's saying, Doc?"

"Hell if I know. And I'm too busy to check."

The sheriff looked at the other survivors. "Can any of you tell me about this?"

"Name, rank, and serial number, boys," Koestel said.

"Ok, I'll bite," Mrs. Kraus said. "What are your serial numbers?"

◇◇◇

While Heather watched her uncle play with the puppy she'd persuaded him would not be named Jesus, she tried to decide what to do next. Pam was home from work. Heather had been invited for supper—take-home holiday-special turkey chimichangas Pam had brought from the Sewa casino's twenty-four hour buffet. Huge deep-fried burritos with enough calories to feed all those deputies Heather believed were still hanging around, too. But Heather knew, by staying, she put Mad Dog and Pam at further risk. Not that the psycho wasn't capable of using them against her, even if she left. And there lay the problem. If she borrowed Mad Dog's Mini Cooper and went home or to Brad's or tried looking for the psycho on her own, the sheriff's detectives would follow her. That would make it easier for the psycho to come here again. Though he'd still have to get through Hailey.

She'd listened to the messages on her cell phone. They were all from Brad. There were none from Benteen County. None from her sister at Texas Tech, either. She didn't want to talk to her dad until she was sure the mess she'd been in all day was over. He fretted about her law enforcement career enough as it was, no matter how proud he felt of her for taking it on. And what could her sister do but worry?

Brad's first message had been a reminder she was expected for dinner. His next call suggested she get back to him before she came. That was followed by one in which Brad said they might want to reschedule Heather's introduction to the senator. But he still wanted to see her. And so did his sister. Maybe they could pick Heather up and go out somewhere. Call him.

But she hadn't called. Not yet. She was still trying to figure out how to avoid putting anyone at greater risk. The whole thing was a giant conundrum. No clear answer that she could ascertain.

Hailey curled up on a colorful Mexican rug near the Christmas tree. The pup snuggled into her belly and fed for a moment before falling asleep. Heather wondered where the gray wolf had gone. And the pack, for that matter.

"Just the one puppy," Mad Dog said. He lay on the floor near Hailey and watched. "I looked. Usually, even wolves have litters. But this little guy is the only one."

Mad Dog's face glowed with the delight of a little boy who'd found the gift he hadn't even known he wanted under his tree.

Pam set the table. Three places. It was growing dark out. Time and inaction, Heather realized, were making up her mind for her. Maybe that was for the best.

Her cell rang. Brad. He was special, someone she wanted to spend time with. Maybe her life. Pam and Mad Dog wouldn't mind if she invited Brad to join them here. He could even bring his sister. With all those sheriff's officers out there, wouldn't they be safer here than anywhere else? She snapped the phone open. One way or another, she had to make up her mind about seeing Brad tonight.

"Heather, are you all right?"

"Sure," she said, not certain it was true.

"You've had quite a day. I heard you found the governor this morning."

"Yeah," she wanted to tell him all about it, but not now. And not over the phone.

"Things are crazy here, too. Are you free right now? Can I see you tonight? And Niki…I want you two to meet."

"My car's at headquarters. I'm at Uncle Mad Dog's."

"We'll come get you. I want to meet your uncle and his girl friend. We'll be there as quick as we can. Okay?"

"Yes," Heather said, and decided it would be okay. Then she folded her cell closed and found Hailey staring at her in a way that made her wonder if the wolf knew better.

◇◇◇

Not only had it gotten dark during the sheriff's adventures, it had begun to snow again. The perpetual Kansas wind made it seem to be snowing sideways. It took the sheriff a few moments to find the lights and the wipers and get the defroster going full bore. Then he had to rock Mrs. Kraus' old Chevy before the wheels got traction and he could maneuver it through all the vehicles in the lot behind the courthouse.

He turned north, then east on Cherry. He stopped at the next corner, got out, and checked the spot where he'd last seen the Korean War Veteran. The man was no longer there. Someone must have come and helped him home. Or the old warrior had found a way back by himself. Paul Graber was gone, too. Aside from some broken windows, fresh chips in store fronts, and a bit of rusty colored snow, no evidence remained of the little battle that had been fought such a short time before.

In fact, the street looked relatively cheery, thanks to a few twinkling Christmas decorations. The next street over, however, glowed with Chernobyl-like intensity. The sheriff didn't know whether Don Crabtree was home or not. But home seemed like a good bet, since someone had turned his display back on.

Mrs. Walker and her attorney needed the sheriff's attention, but Crabtree had shot up his neighbor's RV, threatened several members of the man's family, and might well be armed again. The sheriff wasn't sure what had happened to the Uzi. Someone had picked it up to carry it to the courthouse for him when he exchanged it for his shotgun. He couldn't remember who. Crabtree's light show seemed like the place to start.

English parked Mrs. Kraus' car in the middle of Plum Street, engine running and headlights on high, pointing into Crabtree's yard. But he didn't go to Crabtree's door first. The sheriff started with Conrad, instead.

"Evening, sheriff." Conrad seemed a little taken aback at seeing the sheriff. Perhaps because he hadn't managed to return to the fire fight. "You get things straightened out at the courthouse?"

"With all those bodies, I'm not sure straightened out is the right way to put it."

"Oh." Conrad didn't ask whose bodies, and the sheriff wondered how many calls Mrs. Kraus must have taken by now from the local rumor mill. Conrad might have more up-to-date information on the militia's losses than he did.

"In the midst of that mess at the corner of the park, I lost track of Don Crabtree and his Uzi. You know if he's over there and whether he's armed?"

"Yeah. He's over there, I think. Pretty humiliated at the way this all worked out. I've got his Uzi. Took it as security against the damages to my property. And so he couldn't change his mind and turn it on us again."

The sheriff nodded. "I'm afraid I'll have to take that as evidence. And because it's an illegal weapon, being fully automatic like that."

Conrad didn't argue. "You need help getting it to your car?" The sheriff was still using his mother's old shotgun as a cane, and limping more now. He'd used his legs in ways they were no longer accustomed to and they were complaining about it.

"No. I'll manage."

Conrad got the gun for him. "It's loaded with a fresh clip, in case you need it. Don is blaming Matt Yoder for what happened to the crèche, so Don apologized to me and promised to pay double all my damages, like I said…."

Conrad was trying to tell him something else.

"Yes?"

"So I promised I wouldn't press charges."

"I see," the sheriff said, though he didn't. "Won't matter, though. He'll be facing federal weapons charges and I aim to go after him for everything I can think of for causing all this trouble."

Conrad shrugged. "Just wanted you to know, in case it made a difference. You need help taking him into custody?"

"No, thanks. Wouldn't want to interrupt your holiday any further."

English stuck the Uzi under one arm, leaned on the shotgun with the other, and headed back to Mrs. Kraus' Chevy. He locked the Uzi in the trunk and continued up the walk to Crabtree's front door. Curtains moved in the living room window. Someone inside knew he was coming. But the sheriff's outlook on the matter had gone from Gary Cooper's Marshall Kane to George C. Scott's General Patton. At this point, he damn well intended to crush any one who resisted. He pounded the butt of his shotgun against Crabtree's door.

"Open up, Don Crabtree. You are still under arrest and I've come to take you into custody."

The door swung in. A subdued Don Crabtree stood inside.

"Won't you have a cup of coffee first?" Edna offered from over her husband's shoulder. "I promise you he's not dangerous anymore."

"Roy Conrad's got my Uzi," Crabtree said. "And Edna went and dumped all the rest of my guns and ammunition in Calf Creek after I brought them back from the courthouse. Did it while I was off surveilling the Conrad place. I feel real terrible about what happened over, there since it was Matt Yoder all along."

"Oh, Daddy. It's not Matt's fault," Crabtree's daughter said.

That brought a little of the fire back. "Not his fault? Then who pissed all over my lawn this morning? Look at it. Just look at it." Crabtree marched past the sheriff and out to where the incriminating evidence was gradually being hidden beneath a fresh coat of snow.

"Don," Edna said, following him, "are you telling me after all these years you still don't recognize your own daughter's handwriting?"

Crabtree froze as solid as the icicles on baby Jesus' chains. His gaze slowly turned on his daughter, who was suddenly blushing brightly enough to compete with the lawn decorations.

"Are you telling me that you...? That he stood there and you aimed his...?"

"How old is your daughter?" the sheriff asked.

"She turned sixteen last month," Edna said.

The sheriff was surprised. She looked younger. He'd been sure she couldn't be more than fourteen. But the years flew by him these days. The kids were always older than he remembered.

"I can make an arrest in this matter if you want. But the questions of whose...uh, penmanship is represented and what writing instrument was involved will become public record. It's up to you."

"No harm done," Don Crabtree said. "Just a prank."

The sheriff thought about mentioning the day's count of dead and wounded.

"Sheriff," Crabtree said. "I think I'd like to go to jail now, if you don't mind. Before I kill my only child with my bare hands."

◇◇◇

"Ready, Niki?" Brad called.

The day had stayed cool, though the clouds that kept the sun from warming Tucson and brightening the Coles' family holiday provided a spectacular sunset. Most of the color had bled from the sky by the time Brad let his BMW creep away from the garage and his sister's extended farewell with their father.

"Coming," she called, though she turned back to the senator with a few soothing words, a big smile, and a quick kiss.

It was getting cold for top-down riding, but Niki had asked him to leave it down and Brad knew the heater could do a surprising job of keeping the interior bearable. At last, Niki came running, jumped in, and fastened her belt. "Away, James," she said.

Brad put it in reverse and released the clutch. And damn near plowed into the grill of a monster SUV that had just entered their driveway. Niki's head snapped back against her headrest.

"What…" she began. But she knew what, because blinding headlights peered over the BMW's trunk.

"You should sue for whiplash," Brad said. "I know a good lawyer."

He turned in his seat and called toward the SUV. "Could you back up and let us by, please? We'll be out of your way in a minute."

He was surprised when the vehicle didn't move. The door opened and a figure came striding toward him out of the dazzling light.

"Sorry, Brad," a familiar voice said. "I've got some important news for your father. You should hear it, too."

It was one of the last people on earth Brad would have expected to drop by the senator's home on Christmas. Any other day, for that matter. Brad opened his door and got out, extending his hand to Frank Crayne, chairman of Pima County's board of supervisors. The man took it in one of those quick but firm shakes people in politics master—a gesture devoid of human warmth.

Crayne had a young girl with him. Led her by the hand, though she seemed reluctant to follow. What was that about? Crayne didn't have any children.

The senator admired Crayne. He ran the county like his own private kingdom. But the senator was a Republican and Crayne, though hardly less conservative, represented the Democratic machine that ruled the second most populated county in the state of Arizona.

"It must be important for you to come here personally," Brad said.

"Sorry to delay you," another voice said. This one came from the other side of the car. The speaker had opened Niki's door for her. "We'll try to make this quick."

He was a small guy, handsome, and he moved with a kind of supple grace. Niki noticed it, too, if the gleam in her eye and the hand she extended for him to help her from the car were indications.

The girl with Crayne nodded at the guy on the other side of the car. Raised her eyebrows a few times, as if she were trying to tell Brad something.

The senator walked briskly from where he'd stood by the open garage door. If you didn't know he'd been drinking all afternoon, you couldn't tell it from his gait. Or his breath, unless you were attuned to the near absence of odor left by very good vodka.

"Frank," the senator said as he and the chairman exchanged one of those handshakes and the chairman continued to hold onto the girl. "What brings you here?"

"You know about what's been going on today?" Crayne said. The senator nodded. "Well, there's more. You need to be briefed."

"Yes. I do." The senator glanced at the small man who stood with Niki. "Is this the man who's going to brief me? And who's that adorable child with you?" The senator could turn on the charm when he thought it might benefit him.

Crayne took the lapel of his western-cut-corduroy sports coat in his free hand. Two-handed, it would have been his trademark gesture when he wanted people to know the gravity of what he was about to say. His green-flannel shirt matched the green of his eyes. "Senator Cole," he said, "let me introduce you to Mr. Smith. He's about to change your life forever."

"I beg your pardon," the senator said, confused. Brad didn't get it either. And Niki's look had gone from appraising to concerned. That was when Brad realized the Smith guy continued to hold his sister's arm with a firm grip. And that his sister had decided she didn't want to be held. Neither did the girl with Crayne, Brad realized. And she looked faintly familiar.

"What's going on here?" Brad said.

Smith looked at him and smiled. "You're Brad Cole and you're involved with Heather English. Does she love you?"

"That's none of your business."

"Business?" the little man said. "No, not business. Pleasure. For your sake, and your family's—especially for your sister's and this child's—you'd better hope she loves you more than life itself."

◇◇◇

"You have daughters," Don Crabtree said from the back seat of Mrs. Kraus' car. His hands and ankles were securely duct taped. "How did you survive two teenage girls?"

The sheriff didn't bother trying to explain. For him, half the battle had been remembering how he'd felt as a teenager. Empathizing instead of criticizing.

Instead, the sheriff concentrated on what he still had to do. "Don, who did you tell about me having your guns?"

"Not that many, really. You got to realize, you left me defenseless. I was trying to borrow a weapon off of someone. The Conrad boys coulda come across the street…. Well, I guess, being innocent, they weren't likely to do that, were they? But I still felt threatened."

"I need to know precisely who you spoke with and exactly what you told them. And why you told people I had federal agents helping me and that we were rounding up every gun in the county."

The sheriff glanced at the rear-view mirror and watched Crabtree squirm.

"Well, on account of being humiliated to admit how I lost my guns so easy, I may have exaggerated how you did it to a couple of people."

"Did you mention federal agents?"

"I might have. But by then, the word was already out."

Crabtree looked out the window and realized they were going south toward the old downtown. "Say, where are you taking me?"

"What do you mean the word was out?"

"Well, I got the idea about you having help from federal agents on account of Aunt Lottie."

"Your Aunt Lottie, that would be Mrs. Walker, my neighbor on Cherry Street?"

"Yeah. She called right after you left with my guns. Said you shot up her car and wanted to take her guns, too. That you and a bunch of federal agents had chosen today—Christmas—to begin the Obama gun seizure we've been hearing was coming ever since that Muslim socialist was elected."

"Mrs. Walker told you that?"

"She did. She was real mad at you. I think she may have called some other folks, too, because everybody I talked to asking for the loan of a gun had already heard about it. And several people called me, wondering if it was true about you and the feds seizing my guns."

The sheriff turned right a block north of the railroad tracks.

"Ah, where are we going? Why aren't you taking me to jail?"

"We don't have a jail at the moment, so I'm afraid you'll have to tag along with me. I need to have some words with your aunt's attorney."

"Oh," Crabtree said. "Then I guess you already know about him spreading that same story."

◇◇◇

The professional ushered them all into the Coles' living room. They had been very cooperative, especially after he showed them he now had the county manager's hand gun. The room contained a large couch, a rocker, and several easy chairs. Everyone sat, when he suggested it. Even Mrs. Cole, though she was a bit wobbly and nearly missed the cushion she aimed for. Still, the scene—all of them gathered about a partially decorated tree with the windows providing a spectacular view of the nearby Santa Catalinas fading into dusk—might have been cheery but for the gun.

"Frank," the senator asked the county manager, "why have you brought this man to my home?"

Frank Crayne, moving with appropriate caution, eased his jacket open. He was wearing a complicated harness holding some sort of apparatus over his prominent abdomen.

"What is that?" the senator asked, "a concealed-carry holster for another of your hand guns?"

"No," the professional said. "It's an explosive device."

"A bomb?" The senator, for all his effort to preserve his dignity and demonstrate his importance, seemed suddenly on the verge of panic.

"A shaped charge," the professional explained. "Voice activated and very sophisticated. I only have to speak a certain command to blow a hole through Mr. Crayne's digestive tract. There's one on the girl, too. No need to be concerned, though. The charges are quite precise. No one else will be hurt if I'm forced to use either of them. Though you may find yourselves soiled by blood and whatever they've been eating recently."

The girl opened her jacket. There was a similar harness and device underneath.

"What do you want with us?" Brad Cole had worked up enough nerve to demand information. The professional was pleased. Heather English deserved someone with a bit of courage.

"I thought I already made that clear, Brad. I want your girlfriend. I want Heather English."

"Why? And what does she have to do with us?"

"I'm here because of your father's choice of friends and support, Brad. If you objected to them, maybe you should have made that clear earlier. Or at least found your own clients instead of living off the ones he refers to you."

"That's not fair," Niki said.

Brad sputtered, but remained silent, disappointing the professional. "Then Heather hasn't told you about me?"

Brad shook his head.

"I'm a professional assassin. Heather and I met a few years ago. I accepted money to, shall we say, damage her. She proved to be more skilled and luckier than I expected. She is the only contract I've ever accepted and failed to deliver. So, even though the purchaser of that contract betrayed me and had to be eliminated, I want to put things right. A matter of honor, you might say. "

"That has nothing to do with us," Brad said.

"Of course it does. Heather and I have unfinished business. And very little time in which to complete it. You do recognize the young lady who accompanied Mr. Crayne and myself to your home, don't you? She's Cassie Hyde, daughter of your late governor-elect."

Cassie nodded. She had all but attached herself to Niki after they'd entered the house and Crayne and the professional released their grips on the pair.

"I had planned," the professional said, "for Cassie to be safely in the custody of law enforcement by now, but some people made a mistake. One they will not repeat. Now, here she is, an unwanted complication I will turn into an asset. I want Heather to come to me. She won't want to do that. She may be more likely to agree because I have Cassie. She will be still more likely because of you, Brad."

"I won't help you," Brad said.

"Yes, you will. Not for yourself." The professional turned to Crayne. "Frank, I want you to remove the device you're wearing and go put it on Brad's sister."

Brad jumped to his feet but the professional had sidled in next to Niki. The muzzle of his pistol brushed her temple. "You see, Brad, you'll help because you have no choice. And, if Heather English feels anything for you, she'll come for exactly the same reason."

Brad didn't sit again, but he didn't move. Not even when the Pima County chairman finally succeeded in removing the device and began strapping it around Niki's torso.

"I want you to call Heather now, Brad. I don't care what you tell her about the situation you've found yourself in. It won't matter. I only want you to tell her to meet us at Hi Corbettt Field in Reid Park. In an hour. Will you do that for me Brad?"

Brad refused to answer, but he picked up a phone.

◇◇◇

The sheriff parked Mrs. Kraus' Chevrolet in front of a two-story brick building in what had once been downtown Buffalo Springs. A weathered sign over the door read, ELDRIDGE BEAUMONT, ATTORNEY AT LAW. And, in the window, another—REDUCED RATES ON BANKRUPTCIES & FORECLOSURES. Beaumont owned the building—office downstairs, apartment above—which would have been more impressive if the buildings on either side hadn't been boarded up and vacant for decades. In most downtowns, this would be prime real estate. In Buffalo Springs, it was about as cheap as you could get.

There were lights on behind the window shades, upstairs and down. And Beaumont's car occupied a nearby parking space, a good indication he was home and alone, since no other cars were parked on the block. Or practically anywhere in downtown Buffalo Springs, for that matter.

"You gonna leave me out here in the cold?" Crabtree whined.

"Shouldn't be long."

"What if he shoots you?"

The sheriff turned and looked over his shoulder at the spot Crabtree occupied on the back seat. "Something make you think he might do that?"

"Well, he's involved with that bunch down at the courthouse. Wrote up our charter. I've seen him at meetings...."

"You attend their meetings?"

"We're just a bunch of nice folks who believe in our right to bear arms, sheriff. Nothing wrong with that. We have occasional 'Locked and Loaded' picnics and burn up a little ammunition. Nobody gets hurt."

"Three dead today," the sheriff corrected him. "Don, maybe you better tell me who else is involved in your little social club."

"The Free State Militia is not a social club," Crabtree said.

"I already know most of your members. They're either dead or under arrest. I just want to know who else might constitute a threat, Don. And thanks for the warning about Beaumont."

"I've never actually seen Beaumont carry," Crabtree said. "Or shoot, for that matter."

"I'll keep that in mind," the sheriff said. "But who else?"

"I've said too much already. We're not supposed to tell."

"Sort of a secret society," the sheriff said. "You don't happen to wear sheets, do you?"

Crabtree wouldn't meet the sheriff's gaze as English got out of the car.

The sheriff gimped his way to the attorney's door, still using the shotgun as a cane, mainly because he thought it would be foolish to leave the weapon behind with Crabtree. Even a duct-taped Crabtree.

The front door was unlocked, so the sheriff simply walked in. This was an office and open to the public, or so the sign on the front door said. Beaumont probably never bothered turning it around. That could prove handy in case the sheriff spied his missing files within—no search warrants being required when an officer entered public spaces.

There was a little bell on the door and it rang with a tone more cowbell like than evocative of the holiday. Beaumont came trotting down the stair. "Yes?" he said. And then he saw the sheriff and the color left his face.

"You look like you've seen a ghost," the sheriff said. "Is that what you expected me to be by now?"

"I thought...," the attorney stuttered, "...that is, I heard.... Well, everyone knows about the shoot-out, Sheriff. I'm delighted to see you survived it."

"Yes. It was kind of you to drop by the courthouse in the middle of everything to take my file on your client's case into safe keeping."

"File, Sheriff? I'm afraid I don't know what you're talking about. I did drop by to see if my cousin needed any legal advice for himself and his men. But I assure you...."

"Destroyed it, already, huh?"

Beaumont spread his hands in aggrieved innocence. "Sheriff, really."

"And if Koestel's your cousin, does that mean Mrs. Walker's your aunt, too?"

"You really shouldn't have shot Aunt Lottie's car, you know. We shall almost certainly have to sue. The vehicle was an irreplaceable classic."

The sheriff leaned against the wall and raised the shotgun a little. He felt like using it to blow a few holes through this twerp's collection of framed diplomas.

"Have at with the lawsuits," the sheriff said. "You know what a collection of witnesses I had, and will have again, to the chaos your aunt created."

"I've been speaking with many of those good people, Sheriff. I think you'll find they've reconsidered. That they're convinced my aunt's vehicle was defective. A stuck accelerator pedal, perhaps. And that she bravely managed to keep her car from causing greater damage. That she was, in fact, in the process of bringing it back under control when you lost your temper and opened fire."

"Are you shitting me?"

"Don't threaten me with that gun, sheriff."

The sheriff was not having a good Christmas. He felt like beating the attorney over the head a few times with the Remington. "Have you been bribing witnesses, Mr. Beaumont?"

"You should be cautious of slanderous accusations, Sheriff. Every last person you interviewed will deny your wild charges."

"And how do you know who those people are, unless you stole my file?"

"Uh, well, I was there, of course. I saw who you spoke to."

"Yes," the sheriff said. "But you didn't see the ones I spoke to after I sent her home in your custody."

"There weren't any others," Beaumont began. But then he saw the triumphant look on the sheriff's face and realized the only way he could know that. "Or so I've been told," he said, trying to salvage the moment.

The sheriff pulled out his roll of duct tape and recited Miranda again. It was becoming a traditional favorite this

Christmas. "Come along, Mr. Beaumont. Your cousin, Mr. Crabtree, is waiting for us outside and needs legal advice. You can supply that of course, but not representation. I'm afraid you're going to have to find another profession, following your jail term and disbarment."

◇◇◇

Heather was glad Mad Dog was more interested in spiritual clues than physical ones. The smile she forced when she asked to borrow his Mini Cooper felt more like a grimace. Mad Dog didn't notice. He accepted her story about needing to give Brad a ride and handed her his key. Pam would have noticed, but she'd put the chimichangas in the oven while she got out of her little black dress—her work clothes—showered, and changed to denims.

"I won't be long," Heather said, slipping out the door.

"Not a problem," Mad Dog said. "We're not going anywhere tonight."

Heather popped the electronic lock on the Mini's doors and pulled the driver's one open. Hailey jumped in ahead of her. Heather would have sworn the wolf was still at Mad Dog's side when she left the house.

"Get out, Hailey. You can't help me with this. You've got a baby to bring up."

Hailey didn't move. Her eyes were locked on Heather's as if the wolf was trying to communicate somehow.

Heather reached out to grab Hailey by the scruff of her neck. In a flash, Hailey's teeth closed on Heather's hand. Gently. Well, not quite gently. The wolf continued to stare as she squeezed Heather's hand enough to hurt.

"Let go of me, Hailey. You know I have to do this."

And just like that, Hailey did. The wolf jumped out of the Mini and trotted to the edge of the porch, sat, and looked back at Heather.

"What was that about?" The car's courtesy light revealed tooth marks on both sides of Heather's hand. No broken skin, but Hailey had evidently objected to the idea of being removed from the car. So why had she gotten out, then? And why sit there, wagging her tail?

Heather didn't have time to consider it. She had to get to Reid Park, and she had to figure out whether she wanted those sheriff's detectives out there to follow her.

No, she decided. The threat to Brad and his sister and Cassie Hyde would be too great if the psycho saw them coming. He'd let everyone go as soon as he finished with Heather. He'd promised and she believed him. So she had to make peace with herself. Get ready to die. That, or psych herself up enough to believe she could actually win this fight. Winning would keep Brad and the girls safe, too. And she'd get to live to enjoy it. Wouldn't that be great? Too bad she couldn't convince herself it might happen.

She wanted to go lights-out and fast. But, though the Min was built for speed and cornering, it wasn't built to blend in. She'd get stopped and hauled in for questioning if she tried something like that. Another argument to cooperate—to tell them where to find the psycho. It might be the best thing that could happen, except she knew the psycho was too good to be taken easily. And there was no time to bring in experts or establish plans. If Brad and Niki and Cassie died, she'd be to blame. So she stayed at a reasonable speed and pretended not to notice as the unmarked units fell in behind her.

On the road into Tucson, she let them close up and box her in. She waved and smiled and rolled down her window at a stop light to tell them she was just going to meet her boyfriend for a movie at a mid-town multiplex. They nodded, and kept her in the box.

Two blocks from the turn to the theaters at El Con Mall, she threw the Mini into a neighborhood. Cut its lights, hit the accelerator, and let the little car straighten out winding streets. She went away from El Con, and away from the park. In ten blocks she couldn't even see flashing lights anymore.

She took back streets, except for sudden bursts across the corridors. She was close to the park, but the Tucson night screamed with angry sirens. Would he think she'd brought them? Would he cut his losses and eliminate his hostages? Would he even wait for her? She thought he would. She thought he'd take a chance because he wanted her life so badly. She slipped the Mini behind a clump of thick vegetation in the neighborhood just north of Hi Corbett, got out of the car, and ran toward the field.

It was a strange feeling, running to your death. Hoping you wouldn't be too late for it. Was this what heroes did? Saints? Rush to sacrifice themselves? It didn't feel like that to her. She wanted to live. She didn't feel pride in what she was doing. Just terror. And her biggest terror was that she wouldn't be in time.

◇◇◇

The sheriff left the pair of bickering cousins in the back seat of Mrs. Kraus' car. He'd parked in front of his own house, and limped down the street to Mrs. Walker's home. His bad leg was weakening on him, just as Mrs. Kraus had predicted. Even so, Lottie Walker wasn't going to outrun him if she tried to get away.

This time, the sheriff refrained from beating on the door. He pushed her doorbell, instead, and waited in the spot from which she'd finger shot him earlier in the afternoon. He could hardly see his house from her front porch. The snow swirled under one of Buffalo Spring's few working streetlights like sparkling confetti gone mad. Mrs. Kraus' Chevy appeared as a dusky outline between wind gusts.

Mrs. Walker turned on her porch light and opened her door. She had pulled a knitted shawl around her shoulders and looked like an adorable grandmother on the verge of offering hot chocolate and cookies.

"Hello, asshole," she said. It spoiled the image. "Well, come in if you're going to. I don't plan to leave the door open and heat the whole county."

The sheriff went in, leaning heavily on his shotgun.

"Oh, big man, big phallic symbol," she said. "You must be proud."

The foyer contained a hall tree on which hung her winter coat and flowered hat. A framed GOD BLESS THIS HOME needlepoint occupied the opposite wall.

"I'm not that steady anymore," Mrs. Walker said. "You want to talk to me, I'll be in the living room in my rocker. You want to shoot me like you did my car, you'll have time. I don't move fast."

The sheriff wondered how he'd let her take control of the situation. Whatever, he admired the way she'd done it. He propped his phallic symbol against the hall tree and followed her into a room with a cheery fire, beautiful antique furniture covered with antimacassars, and a modern leather rocker-recliner facing one of those high-definition televisions that covered most of a wall. He kept one hand on the butt of his pistol, though. Mrs. Walker plumped the sheepskin atop her recliner and eased into it, looked at him, and smiled sweetly.

"So, Mr. Bumfuck County Sheriff, spit it out. You've already ruined enough of my Christmas."

"I've got several of your nephews in custody," the sheriff said. "I know what you've been up to since I sent you home this morning."

"What, you mean trying to get you killed? You shouldn't be surprised. Do you have any idea what my life will be like if I lose my driver's license?"

"That's a pretty self-centered view. You proved you have no business behind the wheel of a car this morning. We're just lucky you couldn't get enough traction to kill someone."

"I am an old woman, Sheriff. I have no one to take care of me. Do you really want to condemn me to an old-folks home because I panicked for a few seconds this morning?"

"I don't know, Mrs. Walker. I might have considered those arguments and given you another chance. But three people died because you decided the most convenient way to keep your license was to stir up an even bigger panic and get me killed. At this point, I don't think you need to worry about an old-folks home. I think you'll finish your days in prison."

"That's what I think, too. If you live through the day." Her hand came out from under her shawl with a long-barreled pistol. Chrome-plated, and with a muzzle size big enough to do serious damage.

"Sheriff. My husband killed a grizzly bear with one shot from this .357 magnum back in 1952. Since then, I've done the same with a couple of Mexican illegals who had the nerve to think I would give them a ride from Las Cruces to Albuquerque. Unbuckle your gun belt and drop it on the floor."

The pistol would kick like a son of a bitch. As frail as she was, the recoil would probably knock it right out of her hand. Her hand might be frail, but it wasn't unsteady. He'd be dead by the time she lost her grip—no advantage there. He let his police special fall.

"Zekey. Come out of the kitchen and take the sheriff off my hands. I don't want his blood spoiling my carpet."

Zekey tuned out to be Zeke Evans, whose brother Mrs. Kraus had kneecapped at the courthouse.

"Another nephew?"

"My sisters were a fertile lot, and their children have been attentive. Mostly because I'll leave one or more of them a substantial inheritance. Zekey, it seems, under the circumstances."

"What do you want me to do with him Aunt Lottie?" From the look in Zeke's eyes, the sheriff thought the man would have preferred staying hidden in the kitchen, but his hands were equally steady and pointing an Uzi at the sheriff's midsection.

"Take him out in the back yard and send him to hell," Mrs. Walker said. "Then go over to the courthouse and see that Mrs. Kraus follows him. And Doc Jones. When you're through eliminating witnesses, bring your cousins over here to show me it's done. I'll sign a new will in your favor the minute you get back, and advance you the funds to get current on all your debts."

"But there's highway patrol over there." Zeke didn't seem concerned about the unarmed folks, just the ones who might shoot back.

"There are extra loaded clips in the sewing room for your little Jew gun, dear. Take as many as you like."

Zeke patted a bulging jacket pocket. "Nah. I guess I got enough already." He flipped his thumb toward the back of the house. "Come along, sheriff, let's get this over with."

If he were going to hell on short notice, the sheriff thought he'd rather soil Lottie Walker's living room along the way. But he felt sure she'd shoot him. Maybe he could reason with Zeke. A slim chance was better than none.

"Lead the way," the sheriff said.

"Very funny," Mrs. Walker said. "Step back, Zekey, so the sheriff can't grab your weapon. Kitchen's on the right, Sheriff. You'll see the back door. Just go on through. It's not locked. Hell's just beyond."

◇◇◇

Heather reached the entrance. Hi Corbett—field of dreams, nightmares in her case. Home to the Cleveland Indians for decades back when major league baseball's spring training was about getting ready for the season instead of selling still more tickets. The Colorado Rockies moved in when the Indians left and the stadium went through several renovations. Current capacity, 9500—none in attendance tonight. Earlier this year, big league baseball abandoned Tucson for a better deal elsewhere. Just as, one day, it would abandon those fans.

Heather wished the psycho would suddenly decide to abandon Tucson. And right now. But she found the gate that led into the baseball complex unlocked, as she'd been told. A small cluster of figures huddled on the infield grass. Another, familiar now, stood closer to a second gate, one that allowed her access to the playing field.

"You only brought an audience of three?" Heather said.

"Easier to handle, and just the ones you might risk your life for. Your lover, of course. His sister, because she means so much to Brad. And Cassie Hyde, because she's a child, and because you won't want her to suffer more than she already has."

Heather's current trainer had been trying to break her of sticking to the formal patterns of the martial arts she'd learned. He argued those patterns made your every move more predictable. And so, though Heather was trying to center herself, she nodded at Brad, reassured Cassie, and told Niki she was glad to meet her, though she'd have preferred different circumstances.

"I noticed you've strapped something on each of them," Heather said. "Explosive devices, I assume."

"Yes, voice activated, perfect for hands-free demolition. And complicated harnesses that take a few minutes to remove. No one can run or interfere."

"The usual rules?" Heather had begun pacing, stretching, getting a feel for the grass and the soil underneath. One foot hit something hard in the first-base-line dirt between foul territory and fair. Something metal, where the base might attach. She didn't let herself react to it. It was knowledge—something he may or may not know. Something she might be able to use to her advantage. She didn't let herself dwell on how desperately she needed things like that.

"Yes," he said. "The usual rules. No rules."

"Since in a few minutes it won't matter, will you tell me who you're killing for and why?"

"Oh, Heather. Nothing is real. It's all for show. Entertainment for the masses so they don't notice what's really happening. So the public continues to bicker over silly gut-issues and ignore important ones while the rich get richer. Fools and their democracy, Heather."

Heather didn't know whether he was telling the truth or spreading bullshit. "So you won't tell me."

He lowered his voice. Only she could hear. "Okay. Todd Boursin."

Todd Boursin was the loudest voice in America's hate media. But just a windbag. Only a few crazies actually took him seriously.

"The man who bills himself as the Founding Fathers' Gift to the First Amendment planned this and arranged the financing because Hyde was actually going to try to close the border. This is theater, Heather. Boursin cries out for a closed border, but he and his friends make billions off the drug trade and illegal immigration, and even more from the anger he generates over both. But you'd never be able to prove it because there are a host of bag men and Nixon-like plumbers between Boursin and your locals. Besides, you won't survive the night."

She sighed. He was probably right. "You promise you'll let them go when it's over?" She shouldn't have put it that way. Or should she? He expected to win. If he thought she was resigned, it might make him overconfident.

"They can take the devices off as soon as we're finished. Leave as fast as they want."

"What if I don't trust you?"

He laughed because there was only one answer to that. The one he gave her and the one she wanted to set in her mind. "Then win."

Her pacing had brought her close. Close enough to score a hit.

Kick. Kick. Hand strike. All blocked. Leg sweep. Same, and he smiled because she had been audacious but he'd been ready. And then, because it broke the pattern, just a plain old-fashioned football-style kick to his shin. He spun away from it but it caught him in the calf and he stumbled.

She went after him with everything, then. A chop to his face, a twisting blow to his throat. Kicks, again. And all blocked, though closer. And then he came for her. An open hand strike that would have driven her nasal cartilage into her brain if she hadn't thrown herself into a backwards summersault, grabbing his hand and pulling him after her. She tried to put a knee in his crotch, and he tried to put his other hand's fingers in her eyes. What she expected. What he expected. She hit the ground, at the edge of the base path. He would roll over her. His head would strike somewhere near that bit of metal she'd found. On it, if she were very, very lucky.

Midway through their roll, his hand not quite in her eyes, another break in form occurred to her. She snapped her head forward, opened her mouth. Bit his fingers, just as Hailey had suggested. And she held on as her head hit the ground harder than it should. The bounce added to the force of her bite.

Normally, they would both have rolled back to their feet and pivoted, each trying to go in an unexpected direction, get there first, gain some advantage. Instead, their rolls couldn't be completed. Not until he tore his fingers from her mouth. He left flesh. Blood. She spat it into the grass and spun aside to keep from rolling on top of him where he could end it with a crippling strike.

Heather's recovery was awkward. It took a tiny moment too long to locate him. Another moment to understand what she saw. The kind of lost time that should have killed her.

Cassie Hyde had pounced on him. She pounded his face with a little fist. Once, twice, before she took a strike that threw her violently aside. But the psycho didn't recover his feet. His hands didn't move to defend himself. They clawed at his right eye. His face was dark with flowing blood. More than could be accounted for by the damage Heather had done to his hand.

Heather jumped. Came down on his face. Not a move she'd learned in any dojo. Both feet. Landed hard. Heard him scream. Felt an ankle turn and one of his hands grasp the other. Fell, and kicked again. Hard. In his face again. Felt him let go.

She scrambled back to her feet. His legs kicked, but not at her. His feet pounded the ground. His hands raked his eye. A trick? She didn't think so. Her ankle started to buckle. Pain. Enough to make her scream as well. But there were lots of screams. And her ankle held. She kicked him in the chin. Punted his head hard enough to clear an outfield wall. Did it again. Again. Again.

His body moved with the force of each kick. Didn't move to defend itself. And when she stopped, simply didn't move at all.

Heather remembered Cassie.

Niki held the girl. Brad held Niki. But the child spoke to Heather.

"Tell Mad Dog I found another use for my safety pin." It was all Cassie managed before the light went out behind her eyes.

◇◇◇

The sheriff opened Mrs. Walker's back door. There was a little porch out there, accumulating snow. Nothing else. No trees. No bushes. No place to hide.

"Zeke, are you willing to kill people just so a senile old lady can stay in her home and drive a car?"

"Shut up, Sheriff," Zeke said. "We both know it's more than that now. According to the law I'm already guilty of felony murder."

The sheriff had hoped Zeke didn't know. English had also hoped his posse might have reformed to meet Zeke at Mrs. Walker's back door with their weapons cocked and ready. Instead, there was just a big empty yard filled with snow deep enough to make a dash for freedom extra difficult. His legs weren't likely to cooperate in a dash, anyway. On his right, some rusty gardening tools hung against the back wall. A shovel was in reach, maybe, and the sheriff was short on options. He lunged for it. Got the handle. Pivoted and swung. The shovel's head came off and flew into the back yard. Its handle missed Zeke by enough of a margin that the missing head wouldn't have made a difference.

"What did you do that for?" Zeke let off a burst and the sheriff went over backwards, stumbling down the stairs. He landed hard. Sharp pains. It took a moment for him to realize he hadn't been shot. He'd just landed on the woodpile.

Zeke Evans stepped to the edge of the porch. "One more," he said. "For the coup de grâce she taught us we should use."

The Uzi tore another hole in the darkness.

"I've had enough," Zeke said. "Even keeping our farm isn't worth this. I'm going back in there and I'll take her gun away. She's my fault. And my family's."

"I don't understand," the sheriff said.

"I guess I'll be going to jail for a long time," Zeke said. "Her, too, though she won't live that long. I'll call you when I get her gun. Then you can come in and arrest us."

"Wait," the sheriff said. Zeke opened the back door and went inside again, in no more mood to obey the sheriff's instructions than the average citizen he'd met today.

The sheriff climbed to his feet, not as easily as he might have this morning, and made it to the door in time to hear the boom of Mrs. Walker's .357. Then a short burst from Zeke's Uzi. Then silence. Except for the Kansas wind. After a lifetime, one apparently not over yet, the sheriff no longer noticed.

He opened the back door. "Zeke," he called. No answer. "Mrs. Walker?" Still no answer. He retraced his path to her living room.

Zeke lay in a pool of blood, the exit wound in his back big enough to stick a fist in. Mrs. Walker still sat in her rocker. And it seemed the sheriff had been wrong about how frail she was. At least she'd managed to hold onto the .357 when she shot Zeke. Two hands, and now her steady grip had found another living target.

"No," the sheriff shouted.

Lottie Walker paid no more attention than anyone else.

◇◇◇

Cops everywhere. And I'm one, Heather told herself. The feeling wasn't being reciprocated.

"You claimed you didn't know where this guy was," a Pima County detective said. "So why'd you ditch us to meet him here?"

Heather just told it the way it happened. Over and over. To one law enforcement agency, then another.

Brad and Niki had been led elsewhere. To undergo questioning, too, she guessed.

And then a familiar face appeared. He stepped in and brushed one of the more obnoxious county detectives aside. "Sergeant Parker, TPD," she said. "We're not only inside the city limits, detective, this is city property. My turf, so my turn. Back off and leave us some space."

Parker led Heather into right field. "You all right?"

It was the first time anyone had asked. Heather's arms and legs were sore from blocking blows. Her ankle throbbed and her head hurt from its awkward collision with the ground. She couldn't wait to get hold of a toothbrush and mouthwash to rinse the taste of him away. But nothing was broken, and she was alive.

Being alive surprised her. Elated her. Left her nothing to complain about.

"I'm fine. But what about Cassie? What about the psycho? Did I kill him?"

"Cassie has broken ribs and a collapsed lung, I understand. Some other injuries. But she's young. They think she'll be fine."

"That's a relief."

"Your psycho is dead. You broke his neck. And I understand they found a safety pin in his eye. Somebody drove the tip all the way into his brain."

"Cassie attacked him with the safety pin. Probably saved my life. Then I stomped on his face, maybe drove it deeper."

"I hope it hurt," Parker said. "I hope he had time to suffer before he died."

"Yeah," Heather said. "It hurt. I heard him scream for his mother, or at her. It was confusing, and I think we were all screaming by then. The sirens came right after that. Officers flooded the field. EMTs, a few minutes later. How'd you get here so fast?"

"The fool thought it was safe to leave Senator Cole and his wife with Frank Crayne. Thought they were too involved to go to the police, and too frightened of what he might do to their children. Crayne sure tried to talk them out of it. But the senator let us know. Told us about the bombs and Hi Corbett. So here we are."

"You. You're here because of those bombs he strapped to them, right? I didn't think of that."

"Yeah. Simple devices. We've got them contained."

"And Brad and Niki, they're okay?"

"Physically, anyway. Pretty shaken, but who wouldn't be?"

"I'd like to see them. Brad, especially. Any chance of that? Or am I going to end up answering questions for the next couple of weeks while they decide whether I was in league with the psycho or one of his victims?"

"Oh, you'll tell your story to every law enforcement agency in the state. Feds, too. But it turns out Frank Crayne was in this up to his elbows. And Senator Cole took money to respond to events properly. Both their careers are over. At least Cole spoke up to save his kids. Crayne, I hear, folded as soon as they promised not to seek the death penalty for him."

"Crayne? Pima County Board Chairman Frank Crayne?"

"Bingo. And Crayne is saying your psycho was hired to ramp up anti-immigrant sentiments by bringing Mexico's drug war over the border. That he went along because the resulting outrage would close the border for sure."

Did that make sense? "I asked the bastard what this was about," Heather said. He told me it was all make-believe. Something to distract the public. He said Boursin is behind this. That this was all a fraud to keep drugs and illegals flowing while Boursin and his billionaire friends get richer and more powerful."

"You're kidding? Todd Boursin?"

"Do you think he can be linked…?"

"I don't know," Parker said. "Crayne's talking about phone calls from important people in both parties hinting at what should happen here. Followed by sacks of cash that appeared on his office desk. I don't think Crayne knows anything about Boursin, but if the killer implicated him, we'll try."

Heather remembered what the psycho told her about plumbers and bag men. "It's what he said, but I don't know if it's true. Right now I don't care. I'm just glad it's over."

"Me, too, kid," Parker said. "And I'm glad this drug war was artificial. We'll shut it down before things get too far out of hand. Thanks to you."

"Me? I just reacted."

"Yeah, but you kept the bad guy here. You forced him to put himself at risk. And you stopped him. He'll never hurt anyone again."

"Me and a little girl. With some advice from a wonder wolf."

"Say," Parker said, "that reminds me. Is Mad Dog…?"

She didn't get any farther. Captain Matus advanced across the field assuming firm command. "She answers no more questions. Officer English needs medical attention and she needs rest. Anybody who wants to question her comes through me."

◇◇◇

The courthouse was almost empty when the sheriff got back. A pair of Kansas Highway Patrol troopers got out of their Crown Vic to see who he was when he pulled into the drive. They tensed up when they saw his shotgun, but then he showed them his star.

"I'm Sheriff English," he told them. "Anyone still inside?"

"Your office manager and the county coroner. Everybody else has been transported. Jails or hospitals."

"You boys can take the two in my back seat to a jail for me, if you would. Let's say conspiracy to commit murder for now. I'll get with the county attorney tomorrow and take care of the formalities. Oh, and there's an Uzi in my trunk. I'd appreciate it if you'd take it as evidence, too."

"Our orders are to stay here until this little rebellion is over," the taller one said.

The sheriff nodded. "It is over. I'll sign a document to that effect if that's what you need."

"That'll work," the little one said. "We'll take this pair off your hands. Park your car and I'll meet you in your office for that document after we settle these two in our cruiser."

The sheriff chose a spot the wind had kept free of snow so Mrs. Kraus would have good traction when she left. He didn't want to cart the shotgun around anymore, but he really needed support to get up the steps to the back door and down the hallway to his office.

Doc and Mrs. Kraus met him half way down the hall. Doc took the shotgun and offered to prop up the sheriff with a shoulder. Mrs. Kraus offered the same, though she was too short for more than moral support.

"This patrolman tells us you got the last of them," Doc said. The sheriff had moved so slowly that the officer was already waiting for the document he'd been promised.

"Yeah, sort of." The sheriff sank into the chair behind his desk, found a piece of Benteen County stationery, and signed over his prisoners and the gun and a release of responsibility.

"Thanks," the patrolman said. "You all better get yourselves home now. It's hardly any warmer in here than outside. Go salvage what you can of your Christmases."

Mrs. Kraus agreed. "Yeah, this place hardly even cuts the wind anymore."

The sheriff smiled and nodded. "Merry Christmas" he said as the patrolman crossed the foyer and exited into the snow and darkness.

"So, what happened?" Mrs Kraus asked. "Were those two really the last of our problem?"

"With most of the county armed and ready to go to war over whether they get to keep their guns, I'm not sure. But we should be good for tonight."

Mrs. Kraus appeared doubtful. "What about Lottie Walker?"

The sheriff sighed. "She was behind this whole thing. Some dementia-addled plan to kill me off so she could keep her driver's license and continue to live at home."

"She didn't come to me for a physical," Doc said, "but I've thought her mental faculties were failing for years."

"She and one last militiaman waited for me at her place. She told Zeke Evans to kill me, then finish cleaning up by killing the two of you and those officers who just left. Zeke got me out from under her gun. Saved my life at the cost of his own."

"You mean there's another body I'm responsible for?" Doc asked.

"Two," the sheriff said. "Once she shot Zeke, she had nobody left to take care of you guys."

"Oh!" Mrs. Kraus said, getting it.

"Right. She ate a .357 magnum. In conjunction with Zeke, it made one hell of a mess of her living room."

Doc picked up his bag. "Just what I needed. More Christmas presents to open."

The sheriff held up a hand. "No need, Doc."

Doc Jones and Mrs. Kraus raised matching eyebrows.

"Mrs. Walker told me she was sending me to hell. When she shot herself, it knocked her chair over. Into the fireplace. Her hair caught. So did her shawl. And glowing embers flew all over that room. Old carpet and upholstery caught quick."

"I didn't hear any sirens, Englishman," Mrs. Kraus said. "Didn't you call the volunteer…?"

"Chief of the volunteer fire department was Zeke Evans."

"Oh, my God," Mrs. Kraus said. "I can't think of a single fireman who didn't get shot or arrested today."

"Me, either," the sheriff said. "Her house isn't close to any others. No trees or brush in her yard. And the wind's blowing straight into empty lots behind. So I warned the neighbors, turned off the gas and electric at the meters in the alley, and let it burn."

"I'll be damned," Doc said, walking over to the window. "Come look," he said, "even through all this snow."

They did. The fire blazed like a bright new star, rising in the east.

◇◇◇

Heather crossed the Hi Corbett parking lot with Captain Matus. Brad stood beside a Pima County Sheriff's unit. Niki sat in the back seat, talking intently to a female officer.

Heather couldn't help herself. She ran to Brad. Threw her arms around him and held on tight.

"Oh, Brad. We're alive. We're all of us alive and…." It only took a moment to realize Brad wasn't hugging her back. She stepped away, looked in his eyes. "Are you all right? Did something happen to Niki?"

"Are you kidding?" Brad's voice was husky with anger. "Niki and I just watched you kill a man. A man who came into our home and strapped bombs on us. And you're asking me if we're all right?"

Heather couldn't believe what she was hearing. "But I never thought…."

"You knew he was out there and you didn't warn me. I don't know who you are, Heather. I never dreamed you'd put me at risk like this. You've ruined my father's career. And mine."

"But I saved…?" She stopped. What was the point? This wasn't the man she'd been falling in love with. And she, obviously, wasn't the woman he wanted.

"Stay away from me, Heather English. Stay away from my family. I hope I never see you again."

◇◇◇

Sheriff English's Christmas was ending, and none too soon. Mrs. Kraus had driven him home. Doc had followed her, and the three of them checked to be sure there was no threat the fire at Mrs. Walker's would spread. The place had collapsed and neighbors with garden hoses sprayed the last of the embers.

"I should help them," the sheriff said, but when he tried to walk down the street his bad leg finally gave out. Doc helped English into his house and gave him a cortisone shot. Mrs. Kraus fixed the sheriff a hot toddy using bourbon he hadn't known was there, and heated a frozen turkey dinner in the microwave.

"I brought this whiskey over for Judy near the end," Mrs. Kraus said. "Thought it might help with the pain, but she couldn't keep it down."

Doc found the sheriff's old walker and set it beside his recliner. Mrs. Kraus got him a quilt. Then the sheriff waved them out the door.

When they were gone, he sat for a few minutes, looking at the blank television screen. He didn't want its companionship tonight. He tasted the turkey and decided to go with the hot toddy instead. He put his hand on *To Kill a Mockingbird* and thought about beginning it again. It was five minutes before midnight, but he wouldn't fall asleep soon.

The phone rang and he picked it up. Answered automatically.

"Sheriff English."

"Hi, Daddy." It was Heather, calling from Tucson.

"Hi, kid. I'm glad you called. You have a good Christmas?"

"Amazing." He heard weariness in her voice. "But I was on duty, remember?"

"Yeah," English said. "It got so boring here that I went to the office. Spent my day working, too."

"Christmas without family gets so lonely."

He agreed. "You sound beat, baby. Are you sure everything's all right?"

"Oh, yeah, couldn't be better. I'm at Mad Dog's. He and Pam have gone to bed. And we do have one piece of good news down here."

"I could use some," the sheriff said.

"Hailey presented us with a surprise today. A puppy. Cute little boy. And we met the sire, I think. A Mexican gray wolf."

"I'll bet Mad Dog wants to name the pup Jesus."

She laughed. "You do know your brother."

He laughed with her.

"If the little guy were mine," she said, "I'd name him for the day I just had."

"What, Humbug?"

"No, Milagro."

The sheriff sensed Heather's miracle had come with a price. And that this wasn't the time to ask about it. "Milagro," he said. "Perfect."

And, finally, for one a brief moment, their Christmas actually was perfect.

Afterword and Acknowledgments

My greats are the children of my niece and nephews. The three oldest will turn twenty before this novel is in print. Time flies. Having failed to develop the kind of normal estate in which they might share, I bequeath them the wealth I've discovered in the joy of writing. And a world filled with problems desperately in need of their immediate attention.

Nothing is eternal. Not even a *Nissimon*. Our Hailey moved on to the spirit world just before Christmas in 2008—after *Server Down* was written but before it was released. The first of my spirit animals who so surpassed the concept of pet, and on whom I based Mad Dog's Hailey, died in 1964. She was a white German Shepherd named Sherry. A pair of eager young German Shepherds, Kacy and Allie, lie at my feet and encourage my imagination as I write this. In them, the mystical spirit of "Hailey" continues. When it's my turn, I hope a crowd of *Nissimona* meets me. I believe in Dog.

The idea for the message left in front of the crèche in this novel comes from a story I heard during my anthropology days. It was published in *Pissing in the Snow & Other Ozark Folktales*, Vance Randolph, Avon Books, 1976. The original joke is very old. The author describes its origin as follows: "Told by Frank Hembree, Galena, Mo., April, 1945. He heard it in the late

1890s. J. L. Russell spun me the same yarn in 1950; he says it was told near Green Forest, Ark., about 1885." Half a dozen other versions and sources of variations of the story are listed in a footnote. The next time you tell a joke, consider that you may, instead, be passing along a folktale.

Thanks to the usual suspects. Barbara, my wife, for putting up with the odd nature of life with an author. Elizabeth Gunn, Susan Cummins Miller, and J. Carson Black are dear friends and my critique group. They help make my novels so much better. Karl Schlesier continues to help me understand Mad Dog's world view, and make sense of this one. As do Jess and Susan and Tony and Mike, and a host of others too numerous to name.

I owe much to Arizona government. Our state now ranks second in poverty and has forced its citizens to vote to tax themselves to maintain even woefully inadequate spending on education while our legislators were too busy to balance a budget. I owe them for deregulation of concealed-carry—anybody, now, anytime and nearly anywhere. We are so much safer, especially since packing in bars has become legal. Indeed, our legislature inspires me as they cut taxes on corporations and the wealthy and pay for it by shutting down Arizona's tourism industry, closing state parks and highway rest stops and trying to institute a law that requires everyone to produce papers or go directly to jail. They have provided me with more material than I will ever have time to use.

In spite of our elected officials, Arizona still has some businesses. One is Poisoned Pen Press. I thank Barbara and Rob for having the dream that has allowed me to pursue my own. And Jessica and Marilyn and Nan, as well as the Posse for keeping that dream alive. It's an honor to be part of it all.

For errors, only gremlins and I are responsible. And perhaps Arizona's legislature.

—JMH
Tucson, by way of Hutchinson, Partridge, Darlow,
Manhattan, Wichita, Sedna Creek, et Tabun,
Albuquerque, and a yellow brick road.

To receive a free catalog of Poisoned Pen Press titles, please contact us in one of the following ways:

Phone: 1-800-421-3976
Facsimile: 1-480-949-1707
Email: info@poisonedpenpress.com
Website: www.poisonedpenpress.com

Poisoned Pen Press
6962 E. First Ave. Ste. 103
Scottsdale, AZ 85251